CL16

or

FATEFUL DECEPTION

When Captain Robert Monceaux, of the Fifteenth Light Dragoons, rescues Miss Lucinda Handscombe from a highway robbery, she piques his interest. Robert cannot stay away from her, and Lucinda becomes attracted to him. When her guardian demands that she accompanies him to Madeira against her will, Robert offers to save her. But, after a misunderstanding, Lucinda runs away. And when Robert eventually finds her, they realise they must learn to trust each other for their future happiness together.

KATE ALLAN

◆

FATEFUL
DECEPTION

Complete and Unabridged

LINFORD
Leicester

Gloucestershire County
Council

British Library CIP Data

Allan, Kate
    Fateful deception.—Large print ed.—
Linford romance library
    1. Love stories
    2. Large type books
    I. Title
    823.9'2 [F]

    ISBN 1–84617–527–5

Published by
F. A. Thorpe (Publishing)
Anstey, Leicestershire

Set by Words & Graphics Ltd.
Anstey, Leicestershire
Printed and bound in Great Britain by
T. J. International Ltd., Padstow, Cornwall

This book is printed on acid-free paper

1

January 1810

For I have sworn thee fair, and thought thee bright, Who art as black as hell, as dark as night.

Lucinda shivered, closed the slim volume and shut her eyes. She rested the book on her lap and her head on the soft brocade.

How much farther did they have to travel today? Mr Ferris had not said. She thought about the sonnet she had just read. She did not fully understand its meaning and yet she had felt stirred by its words. Mr Shakespeare was a clever man, far more clever than even a nineteenth-century young lady who has had the benefit of education.

She was not certain that Mr Shakespeare's sonnets were suitable and had at first hidden the title page

1

from view but Mr Ferris had shown not an ounce of recognition and had said nothing as he sat opposite her watching her read. The carriage jolted suddenly, the horses reared and they came to a crunching halt. Lucinda was thrown forward and fell back again, nearly missing the seat. The volume of sonnets was hurled to the floor. Lucinda reached to pick it up, when she sat up in fear.

What was that she'd heard? A pistol shot? Her skin froze. Prickles of goose-flesh raced up her neck. She sat upright, staring at Mr Ferris. His face was haloed in the double flash of light. He was as pale as chalk. Through the sudden, uneasy silence came the legendary words.

'Stand and deliver!'

Lucinda's heart stopped for a moment, then continued to thud all the more quickly. Who had fired the pistol? Lucinda longed to turn her head to the window and see what was happening but every part of her body remained frozen. Mr Ferris sat as though pinned to the corner. His wide eyes stared straight ahead, fixed on something beyond what was visible. Should he not do something?

The carriage swayed. Lucinda heard the scuffle of horses' hooves and shouting, made incomprehensible by the slicing wind, and the heavy drumming in her ears. There was another stillness, this time punctuated by two voices coming closer to hand. Lucinda closed her eyes, not wanting to see what happened next. If these were to be her last moments on this earth, she wanted to face them blind.

One of the voices was John, the coachman, his country vowels immediately recognisable.

'Sir, miss, have no fear. They have gone.'

The other voice was unknown to her but, although it held a certain burr, it was the cultured voice of a gentleman.

'Sir . . .'

A horse whinnied. The gentleman cleared his throat.

'Your attackers have fled.'

Lucinda opened her eyes. She was still in the slightly dim inside of the coach. It was not all a dream but the menace had vanished for the moment.

'Thank goodness!'

Mr Ferris lost no time giving himself a cursory dust down, pushing open the carriage door and leaping out. Light and gusts of cold, but welcome, air came in. Lucinda found she was shaking as she followed him outside.

Their horses had bolted. John, the coachman, looked helpless, like a babe without its mother, while Mr Ferris glowed red with indignation and cursed under his breath.

'Murderous villains!' he thundered.

It was no band of heroes that had saved them, but one solitary cavalry officer, in full regimentals, resplendent on his handsome black mare.

'Captain Robert Monceaux of the Fifteenth Light Dragoons at your service, sir.'

Lucinda did not know if she imagined it, but she thought she saw a flicker of unease pass like a shadow over Mr Ferris's face. Did he know the gentleman already? It appeared not.

'William Ferris, who will ever be in your debt, young sir. I am afraid that without your timely intervention, my ward and I . . . '

' 'Tis nothing more than my duty, sir.'

'I had heard, of course, that Hounslow Heath was notoriously dangerous, but surely not now. Not in the nineteenth century would I have expected to be accosted by such veritable cut-throats!'

Lucinda stole a glance at the young dragoon captain with the French-sounding name. She could see he was as tall as the authority of his voice suggested, even though he was mounted on a fine horse. He did not sound French, but there was something to his accent she could not place. It had a burr to it suggesting he was from some unknown locality.

His apparel was pristine, without a

crease, his collar as stiff and straight as his back. Only in his eyes was there any softness to temper the unyielding conformity. Oh, and his thick eyelashes and tumbling waves of hair made her think of chocolate! At the same moment as that very thought, he turned as if to appraise her.

'And, miss, I trust you are none the worse for your ordeal?' he asked.

'La, sir, it was nothing!' she heard herself reply lightly, and felt an unwanted blush arise in her cheeks.

Oh, foolish girl, she chided herself, to have a head so easily turned at the prospect of a uniform!

He was speaking to her guardian again now.

'Highwaymen and footpads will always try their chances on an empty road, wherever it may be. Have a care, sir, for although the dragoons do use the heath as a training ground, that is not sufficient to deter the scoundrels.'

'I thank you for your warning,' Mr Ferris said, shaking his head gravely.

'There is an inn about a mile from here. It would be my pleasure to call in there and have them send horses, sir.'

'You are too kind!' Mr Ferris effused, brightening.

Lucinda shivered. It felt very cold, despite her woollen cloak.

'The young lady may ride with me to the inn where she can wait in the warm.'

The captain's voice sounded more like an order than a suggestion. He must have noticed she was cold. Lucinda felt a strange warmth despite the chill of the air.

'Oh, she can, can she?' Mr Ferris immediately retorted, drawing himself up to the full height of his short frame. 'Miss Handscombe is my ward and a lady of impeccable virtue and spotless reputation. I am afraid I am not about to entrust her person into the care of an unvouched-for dragoon.'

The captain nodded.

'As you wish.' His reply sounded gallant, without any trace of emotion.

Why, then, did Lucinda sense a tension in the air that could be cut with a knife? It was very curious. The dragoon had made a gentlemanly suggestion but for some reason her guardian had objected vehemently.

'Thank you,' she said, struggling to stop her teeth from chattering. 'I shall be quite contented waiting here until the new horses arrive.'

The damp evening mist felt as if it was closing in. Oh, to be a hundred miles from this dreadful place and tucked up in a warm, feather bed! The captain was looking at her, just for a moment, before he spoke again.

'Do you wish your ward to catch her death?' he addressed Mr Ferris.

His words sounded like an accusation.

Mr Ferris looked about to reply. His brows had knitted. It was the same indignant expression he had been wearing a moment ago but he tempered it very quickly into a more reasoned expression. There was a harsh edge to his butter-smooth voice and his eyes shone like hard, ebony beads.

'Lucinda, go with the captain.'

She had no business judging her guardian or their rescuer but both were behaving insufferably. She felt like some token of little consequence and yet worthy of squabbling over. It was intolerable!

'Mind you secure a private salon, sir, and I would be obliged if you would wait with Miss Handscombe at the inn until my arrival. I have no confidence in the safety of a young lady alone in these parts.'

'Sir,' the captain replied in agreement.

Lucinda bit her lip, but was unable to stop herself protesting. What was Mr Ferris thinking of to entrust her to a complete stranger? What if the highwaymen were also at the same inn?

'Sir, I cannot go to an inn alone. Really, it is most unseemly.'

'Your modesty and strong sense of propriety does you every credit,' the captain said and Lucinda fell silent. 'These are, however, most exceptional circumstances and the inn is not a mile from here. Every haste will be made to ensure you are parted from your guardian for as short a time as possible.'

His voice sounded kind but it most certainly did not invite further resistance. Her duty was to obey her guardian and there was something indefinable about the captain that invited her to trust him.

Mr Ferris was still simmering and appeared not to be wholly satisfied. Lucinda said nothing and let John help her mount the magnificent mare. It was comforting to be on such a docile and yet powerful animal. What actually disturbed her was the fact that she was practically sitting in the captain's lap!

'Hold on tight,' he instructed.

There was nothing to hold on to apart from him. Lucinda had her reticule clasped tightly in one hand and the captain's jacket in the other. The stiff braid dug into her hand. Whatever the exceptional circumstances, she should not be here, like this, trying to hold on to a man!

'Hold on properly!'

He took her reticule and tucked it into a pocket. She tried to ignore everything around her, but the idea that the highwaymen might be watching them, about to attack at any moment, persisted. If they were set upon, she reasoned, the captain had a pistol. He had defended them already and he would do so again. Besides, the heath was generally open with only small clumps of trees. There was nowhere from where the highwaymen might spring without giving them fair warning.

Lucinda shivered, but not because of the cold. There was an unexpected warmth as her body pressed accidentally against his. A feeling of assurance enveloped her. She was warm and safe for the moment.

They reached the inn all too quickly and the cold air hit her once more on all sides as she dismounted. Lucinda glanced hastily around the inn yard. It was empty, thankfully, and all looked as it should. The lone ostler was watching them with a strange look on his face.

She supposed it wasn't every day that he must see a handsome dragoon with a lady come riding in. Whatever the ostler might think, the circumstances were extraordinary and her guardian had given his consent. She had nothing to be ashamed of.

The captain handed the reins of his horse to the ostler with a few low-spoken words.

'She is in good hands.'

Lucinda started. Was the captain speaking of her? He was standing across the yard, though the distance seemed shorter, and watching her with an expression that looked like curiosity. She knew she did not cut a fashionable dash. Her grey cloak was about as becoming as an old flour sack.

'Miss Handscombe, do you not want to go inside?'

Ah, now that he was assured as to the comfort of his horse, he condescended to consider her!

'Thank you very much, sir.'

Pleased that she was well mannered enough to have been able to suppress any sound of pique in her reply, she followed him obediently with her eyes fixed on the solid frame in front of her. The captain appeared to know the inn well and showed her directly into a small, private sitting-room. It was comfortable enough, well furnished, and with a well-stocked fire.

'Sit near the fire and ask if you want anything,' he commanded and then disappeared.

Lucinda sank into one of the inviting armchairs. She ought to be feeling more wary, having been separated from her guardian and placed wholly in the hands of an unknown dragoon officer. Although the dragoon was indeed a stranger, Captain Monceaux was certainly a gentleman. Even if he was in want of a little polish in his manner towards females, his actions confirmed his integrity.

Her guardian was almost as equally unknown to her. She had been in his company only these past three days and had made his acquaintance less than one week before that. She had seen Mr Ferris to be a man of sober dress but enterprising character. He had a quick mind, faultless in calculations regarding travelling distances, turnpike tolls and such.

Yet Mr Ferris had said very few words to her beyond what was necessary. She knew very little about his family, save that he had a sister, and nothing of his connection to her family. How had Mr Ferris come to be her guardian? He had said nothing on the subject and so she did not know.

Lucinda sat up at the knock on the door. It was only a maid bringing refreshments. Before departing, she restocked the already hearty fire. Its orange warmth seeped through the room and began to dull Lucinda's senses. She had little experience of inns but this one did not seem busy. There was a soft silence, nothing to disturb her.

★ ★ ★

The drizzling mist was clinging to his skin and Robert could feel droplets of water start to run down the back of his neck. Where was Mr Ferris?

This was the spot. He knew Hounslow Heath like the back of his hand. His mount, Armada, shifted uncomfortably and tried to shake her head. Robert smoothed his hand down her flank. She was as damp as he was and no doubt not the happiest to have been recalled from her stable so quickly.

'Come on, girl,' he muttered to her.

At the sound of his voice, she stilled, not so the inn horse he was leading. This one had a skittish look in her eye. Not an inch of sky was visible through the grey above. It would be dark soon. Robert looked up, but knew what the inclement clouds had been telling him since they had set out.

'Sir?'

The ostler was mounted and also leading another horse. Both his animals were also starting to look agitated. They knew the drizzle was about to turn into a full-blown storm.

Back to the inn, then, and the young lady. There was no reason why she should have a mysterious ability to pique him. She was just some school-room chit. He would do his utmost to disregard her.

To be sure, it was ill-luck he had stumbled into this inconvenient obligation. Where had Mr Ferris gone?

Armada was damp, cold and tired, just like himself. There was nothing for it but to go back to the inn . . .

Lucinda did not possess a timepiece and there was no clock in the room, but she knew she had been sitting here for some time. Where had the captain gone? She had obeyed his instructions obediently, fully expecting that, as Mr

Ferris had asked him to wait with her at the inn, he would appear at any moment to join her. Was he taking refreshment in one of the public rooms, or had he gone with the horses to fetch her guardian? What could she do? She did not want to draw attention to herself by wandering into any of the public rooms.

It was growing dark outside. What if she had been entirely abandoned? The captain must still have her reticule and without it, she had not a penny on her. How could she pay for the food? Where could she go? How could she get there? What was going to happen to her?

A crash echoed from outside — thunder, as though someone was taking the sky and was shaking it! It is only a storm, she told herself. Then she jumped to her feet at the sudden sound of knocking at the door. It was the same maid again! Where on earth was the captain?

'What of the captain?'

'Miss, he's gorn abroad, to take some horses to the coach.'

Lucinda had suspected as much.

'There were none else to do it, miss. Will yer be wantin' anythin' else?'

Lucinda shook her head. Her hands were gripped tightly together in her lap. She was alone, abandoned, in the strange inn, in a district proven to be awash with highwaymen and cutthroats.

2

The door was pushed open violently. It was the captain! Relief swept through Lucinda like a cooling breeze.

'Good,' he exclaimed, moving nearer to the fire and peeling off his sodden gloves. 'You are still here!'

'Of course I am still here! Where do you suppose I might have gone?'

The fire threw his profile into a silhouette. What a fine portrait it would make if she had been a competent artist and could have captured with her pencils that easy gaze.

Robert straightened. What a picture — the young girl in her shabby clothes. Her eyes flashed like a pair of diamonds. Was it possible that behind her demure manner and school rags there was a girl of spirit?

Her frown deepened as he spoke to break the awkward silence.

'Well, your guardian has disappeared,' he stated.

'How can that be?'

Robert took care to keep his tone even, measured. She was not a new, recruited dragoon. She was a chit and, for the time being, in his protection.

'I rode to the very spot we left your guardian on Hounslow Heath and there was no trace of him.'

Her eyes seemed to have been doused. They looked dull. He might have expected a bit more resistance. Was she afraid? As a gentleman, he should get down off his high horse and reassure her.

'Do not worry.'

Robert strode over purposefully so that he stood in front of her.

'You still have my reticule,' she said.

Her gentle voice sounded cracked. Was that what was worrying her? Females and their trifles! He drew the bag from his jacket and handed it to her. She stifled a sob.

'What on earth am I to do now, sir?'

'I can see we are in a somewhat delicate situation. Perhaps I might enquire further into your circumstances so that we might discover what the best course of action is.'

'What is it you wish to know, sir?'

'A little as to your destination and situation.'

'Situation? Why, I am a gentle-woman!'

Her reply was most indignant.

'Forgive me. Perhaps I put it badly. What I should like to understand better is your relationship with Mr Ferris.'

'He is my guardian.'

The captain said nothing. Although she had already answered his question, he was looking at her most peculiarly.

'Do you not believe me?'

Lucinda stared back at him, but those thick dark lashes did not even flicker. He folded his arms.

'He has the appearance of a man more in the guise of a lover, rather than a guardian,' he said.

'How so?'

Lucinda found she was more intrigued than cross. Mr Ferris, her beau! What an absurd notion!

'He is protective . . . '

'As any guardian should be!' he interrupted.

'And he . . . he . . . '

Lucinda pursed her lips as the anger now began to rise so swiftly it threatened to choke her.

'Try harder, sir, for so far you have yet to convince me of any truth in your quite impertinent suggestion!'

'He certainly gives every appearance of a man who would wish to be your lover.'

Lucinda stole a look back into the dark intense eyes of the captain and shivered.

'Has it occurred to you, the extreme impropriety of talking to a young lady, an unmarried young lady, and of so short an acquaintance, on the subject of lovers, either real or imaginary?'

'I should not have mentioned it,' he said, bowing in a formal manner.

Lucinda felt a frustrated stab of disappointment as she saw the passion in the captain's eyes replaced by a mask of apparent indifference.

'It is apparent to any observer that when your guardian looks at you, he undresses you, thus.'

The captain gave her such an appraising gaze, up and down from head to toe, that she started to blush. What trickery he employed, she did not know, but how dare he regard her so!

'Sir, desist immediately from jesting with me in this ridiculous and unseemly manner!'

'Quite,' he said, his face still impassive. 'We will return to the matter in hand.'

Lucinda clasped her bag. Her guardian had lost her and now there was no-one else she could ask for assistance apart from the man before her. It was a most vexing, unsatisfactory situation. She must decide now if she could trust the captain. He was sympathetic to her situation and had pledged to help her find a solution. What alternative did she have?

'We were on our way to Richmond,' Lucinda began, desperately trying to make her words sound even and measured. 'I understand it is not far from here. Perhaps it might be possible to secure some transport, a passing mail coach for example, that I might proceed to Richmond without delay.'

'Not at this hour.'

He shook his head and, turning on his heel, moved towards the door.

'But I shall enquire of the landlord. What is the address in Richmond?'

Lucinda bit her lip. She fixed her gaze no higher than the tops of his boots, her voice little more than a whisper.

'I am afraid I do not know.'

The captain's eyes widened.

'As uneasy as I was to entrust you to a public conveyance,' he said, 'now it is completely out of the question as you do not even know where you are bound!'

'I have not above three guineas on my person. I must reach this lady in Richmond and wait for my guardian there.'

Lucinda felt herself tremble.

'We shall get you to Richmond, but what do you propose? That I ride there with you as I did here through the public streets in front of all and sundry?'

'No!'

'Can you ride?' he demanded and waited patiently for her to reply.

'Yes, but . . . '

'Otherwise, it might be possible to persuade the ostler to loan us his dogcart and I could drive you to Richmond.'

'Let us ride to Brentford.'

The captain looked as if he had laughter in his eyes but Lucinda could not tell if he was being serious, and she felt her every move was under scrutiny. She was aware of him as a man in a way that she had never been aware of any man before.

'You may not have noticed, but there is a violent storm raging outside. While I agree that we should proceed to Brentford, as I have proposed, I have no intention in setting out until it has abated substantially.'

The sooner she was back in company, the sooner her firm footing would return. Her throat was dry and ticklish and tears burned at the back of her eyes. Hunger had started to knot her stomach, but she had no interest in the food on the table.

The captain picked up his gloves from where they lay in front of the fire.

'Let me go and see the ostler. I am sure a mount can be found for you.'

Lucinda knew she should be thankful that he wanted to reassure her, but his every sentence seemed contrived to show how much she needed that very reassurance. His every soft word only served to tell her how much she needed that compassion.

Why did she not have the courage to meet it head on, to recognise it, accept it and use it? Had he been trying to cheer her with humour? Why, when he was so kind, did she want to repay him with anger?

She watched his departing figure and turned to stare at the receding amber glow of the fire. She should be grateful that there was a gentleman doing his utmost to secure her continued safety and well-being. Yet what if they were forced to spend the night together at this inn? The captain was no doubt trustworthy as a gentleman, but there was something dangerous in the way that his glance seemed to send her pulses racing.

She used to long for adventure but now that she was right in the middle of the most alarming and exciting adventure that a young lady could ever hope to have, she did not want to be here.

* * *

What a stroke of ill-luck! Robert wished he was a man for cursing, then he could have cursed under his breath. He had now discovered that half a dozen dragoons from his regiment were supping here and at their head was Derry, from C Troop, the fastest eye in the regiment. Derry could shoot a man down at one hundred paces. He was not going to miss the sight of one of the regiment's captains riding off with an unknown female into the night.

'Caught in the storm, too, sir?' Derry asked his captain.

The dragoon who spoke obviously had not yet learned that it did not do to address an officer without being invited to do so first. Robert understood the men were in high jinks to be back home on English soil after what they had been through in France. However, his own circumstances were more pressing.

Robert nodded in their direction. He had acknowledged them and not every officer would have done. He moved past the group, steadfastly ignoring them. They appeared to take it well enough, turning back immediately to their own conversations.

How was he going to get the girl out of the inn without being spotted? If she had a greater resemblance to a woman of easy virtue he would not have minded so much. Although Robert had never been wont to indulge in such pastimes, he was, in theory, quite entitled to take his pleasure where and when it suited him. His charge, unfortunately, was unmistakably straight out of the schoolroom and ill-dressed to boot.

On his return to her room, she was sitting exactly as he had left her.

'There is a suitable mount for you, however, we cannot be seen riding out of the inn together. There are some men from the regiment here.'

She nodded. It was almost imperceptible, but Robert could see she understood. There was a quick mind hidden beneath those hideous garments. He smiled and she loosened the grip on her cloak a little.

He pulled his gloves back on. They

were dry and it was warm as toast in here. How could the girl possibly be cold? Robert frowned — a mistake. She clasped her hands together as if her life depended on it.

'We shall have to leave unnoticed. I will arrange for our mounts to be ready nearby. We will have to creep out separately, on foot.'

'What about the storm?'

'The storm does make our immediate departure somewhat inconvenient. I am concerned, however, at the lateness of the hour.'

Robert swallowed. He had led men into battle. Was he going to be rattled by a mere chit? He gave up only a small amount of ground.

'We will wait half an hour and hope that it passes.'

★　★　★

Having to sneak out of the back of the inn like a thief and then creep along that slippery, sodden path alone in the pitch dark had not been pleasant at all. Lucinda's breath had caught in her throat and her neck had prickled with goosebumps.

The moon was hidden by the clouds and all she could see with any clarity were the black silhouettes of the winter trees against the leaden sky. The vegetation closer to ground was almost impossible to distinguish.

Once she stumbled with alarm and nearly cried out as the wind whipped a stray branch into her face. When she had finally seen the hazy light of a single swaying lantern she was close to tears.

The mount the captain had found for her was a first-rate chestnut mare who sensed her fear but did not even flinch. There was something about riding a fine horse unhindered that was like nothing else in the world! The storm had abated, leaving only light drizzle to hit her face. She was wrapped up warm and dry. Lucinda was now ready to savour every moment.

The captain rode hard just ahead of her, no doubt keen that their journey be as short as possible. Lucinda was pleased to keep up the pace. She was a fair rider although she had never had the luxury of her own horse. She hoped he was pleased to find he could push on faster than he had first anticipated.

They came shortly to Brentford, which was thankfully quiet. The captain trotted into the carriage driveway of a most pleasant large, modern brick house. He dismounted directly at the front entrance and handed the reins to a young lad who had appeared suddenly. She supposed she had better do the same.

By the time she had dismounted, the captain had already sprinted up the broad steps and was knocking on the heavy door. It opened almost immediately.

'We are not expected, but please inform Lady Hastings that Captain Monceaux and Miss Handscombe are here on a matter of the utmost urgency and delicacy.'

Lucinda nearly blushed. It was most unorthodox. It was just as well that she was a young gentlewoman of a mean and lowly situation. Were she a fine debutante, she would no doubt be utterly ruined by what had happened already.

The butler invited them indoors with a certain familiarity towards the captain and without even checking whether or not his mistress was at home. How regular a visitor was the captain to this house?

They were shown into a drawing-room papered in eggshell blue and fashionably furnished in the Chinese style. Oh, her travelling clothes were so dull and outdated! What was the lady of this house going to think of her? Lucinda sat on the darkest-coloured chair she could see, close to the fire.

The captain did not sit, preferring to turn about the room, stopping occasionally to look out of one of the three fine windows, two of which faced to the front. What was he thinking? What had started as a simple act of gallantry had led to the most unexpected consequences. He might have pressing duties back in Hounslow.

Well, Lucinda was not going to deny how glad she felt at his sense of gentlemanly obligation despite her own manners which, at times, had certainly been lacking. Lucinda did not like to think what might have happened were she not so fortunate to have benefited from his generosity.

It was not a long wait before a tall, stately lady with greying hair swept in.

'Monceaux! This is indeed a pleasant surprise!'

The captain duly kissed her hand and gave a small bow.

'Your servant.'

'You have been working far too hard these last few days,' she said. 'I have not seen you since you have been quartered at Hounslow.'

'Lady Hastings, may I present Miss Handscombe?'

There was amusement in his eyes. Lucinda's heart started to beat faster. She wished she could just disappear somewhere. She rose and deferred to the elder lady with a curtsey.

'Miss Handscombe?' Lady Hastings spoke her name very carefully. 'No, I am afraid I have not had the pleasure of your acquaintance.'

'I have spent these last few years in Chippenham, Wiltshire, ma'am.'

'And in the schoolroom, too, I should think, for you barely look old enough to be out of it!'

Lucinda forced a smile.

'I am nearly twenty, ma'am, and was at a seminary for young ladies.'

Lady Hastings regarded her from head to foot. She turned to speak to the captain.

'Robert, will you step outside with me a moment?' She motioned so that he had no choice but to offer her his arm. 'We will not be a moment, m'dear.'

Robert found himself displeased to

have been manoeuvred so skilfully by Lady Hastings into her library.

'Robert, you have arrived at my house with a young lady and a badly-dressed young lady at that! Please explain yourself immediately or I will have no hesitation in writing to your mother to inform her of . . . '

'You may inform my mother as you wish, however, it has no bearing on the matter at hand.'

He would do well to remember that Lady Hastings was one of his mother's dearest friends. Robert wondered if he had miscalculated that Lady Hastings' charity would extend to a stray, unvouched-for chit.

'I am here to ask for your assistance. To be sure, you fear the worst, but I am not trying to execute an elopement or seduction. You have my word.'

Lady Hastings looked nonplussed so Robert hazarded to continue.

'I rescued the chit from a highway robbery earlier this afternoon, on Hounslow Heath. I had never set eyes on her before that moment. I just require to reunite her with her guardian in the most seemly manner possible. Your assistance would be appreciated.'

'You can vouch she is a gentlewoman then?' Lady Hastings smiled. 'Of course, we must reunite her with her guardian!'

Whatever business Lady Hastings had with the captain, surely it could wait a while? Lucinda was glad when they returned promptly.

The captain began the story. Lucinda found herself lulled by the sound of his soft tones. Where did the captain come from with such dulcet vowels? It was a pleasure to listen to him.

Lady Hastings had been listening quietly but when the captain began to describe how he had returned to the heath and found Mr Ferris had disappeared, she interrupted.

'Are you sure your guardian did not come to the inn for you? How very singular that he should disappear like that! No doubt he is scouring the neighbourhood now for his ward. We must get Miss Handscombe home immediately. Where are you headed in Richmond? What is the name of your guardian's sister?'

Lucinda felt herself trembling as she confessed her ignorance.

'I am afraid I do not know.'

'Richmond is not so big a place. Let me see, is she a married lady?'

Lucinda shook her head.

'I am not certain, but I have the impression she may be a widow.'

'Ah! A lady like myself. Well, there cannot be so many in Richmond. Now, Mr Ferris, the name is familiar. Would he be the wine merchant who supplies the royal households?'

'Yes, the very same!'

Lucinda suddenly felt as if a vast burden had been lifted off her. Her guardian was a person known to Lady Hastings.

Lady Hastings dismissed the butler. She looked strangely uncomfortable as she spoke.

'The gentleman is known to me. I am sure we can discover where his sister resides. I shall go and set some enquiries in motion.'

She rose to leave just as the tea arrived, and so poured for them all before leaving the room.

'Lady Hastings is a kindly lady,' the captain said.

Lucinda felt her cheeks burn and to hide it, sipped her tea. It scalded her tongue. She put the cup back down rather inelegantly but that was better than keeping it in her shaking hand. He, at least, was not wholly insensitive to her feelings.

Lady Hastings returned, and said, 'I have not yet been able to discover the whereabouts of your guardian's sister. Your guardian has a house in the City, does he not? I shall send a letter there also.'

Lucinda nodded.

'Now, the hour is very advanced,' Lady Hastings continued. 'We must dine and you must accept my invitation to stay here this evening.'

'Oh, but . . . '

Lucinda bit her tongue. What was she saying? Of course she wanted to stay here! Where else was she to go?

3

I insist on it. Even if we hear back from Richmond this evening it will be very late,' Lady Hastings continued.

'Lady Hastings has an exceedingly comfortable house and you will be quite safe here,' the captain said.

'Thank you very much, Lady Hastings.' Lucinda swallowed. 'I should be delighted to accept your kind invitation.'

Lady Hastings rose to ring the bell.

'Will you stay to dinner, Robert?'

'Oh, but I cannot dine in my travelling clothes!' Lucinda exclaimed before she could stop herself.

The captain had the effrontery to laugh at her!

'I would be exceedingly shocked if you chose to dine out of them.'

'Robert! Miss Handscombe, although you are quite correct to question the propriety of dining in your travelling clothes, I think, in the circumstances, we will not stand on ceremony. I have a day dress that might suit you, though I am a little taller.'

'I am afraid I must bid you good-night.' The captain broke in stiffly. 'I must get back to my men.'

Lady Hastings nodded.

'Well, Miss Handscombe,' he said, 'it has been a most diverting afternoon. I hope you enjoy your stay with Lady Hastings and that you are speedily reunited with your guardian.'

'Thank you.'

There was a painful stab in her chest, like disappointment, at the thought that she might never see him again. She immediately chided herself. The captain cut a fine figure and was brave to have faced their assailants. This was no time, however, to start imagining dancing with him at a ball. Such foolish fancies did nothing but show what a schoolgirl she still was.

'Cut to the chase, for heaven's sake, man!'

Lord Rawleigh drummed his fingers on the bureau.

'We lost both the dragoon and the girl at the inn. They must have sneaked out somehow,' Bill Cunningham replied.

He was an ex-Bow Street Runner who would do anything anyone paid him for.

'What do you mean you lost them?' Rawleigh exploded.

'I had my two men occupied misleading Ferris to the wrong inn and so I had only one man on the girl. She was in a private sitting-room the whole time. My man was in the inn tap-room where he would have seen anyone leave.'

'And what about Ferris?'

Cunningham reached into a deep pocket and drew out a small, leather notebook which he consulted.

'Ferris returned just after ten o'clock

last night to his house in Wardrobe Place, alone.'

'Is someone posted at Ferris's house?'

'Of course.'

'What has the dragoon done with her? And who is he anyway? Don't you think you ought to be trying to find out? I must find the girl.'

★ ★ ★

Lucinda stifled a yawn. Waking up to the gentle winter sunshine and pleasant fire already well underway in the grate was delightful compared to the hospitality they had enjoyed at diverse inns over the last few days. The small clock on the mantelpiece said it was half past ten. Frightfully late!

She pushed back the blankets and heavy counterpane and scrambled out of bed. The water in the jug on the dresser was hot and in the dressing-room next door, Lucinda discovered the promised day dress and other necessities.

Lady Hastings stood to bid her good-morning when she came into the dining-room and suddenly Lucinda found that she was ravenous. The toast was fresh and warm and she was assaulted by a variety of other tempting aromas from the buffet.

'Did you sleep well, my dear?'

'It was so comfortable, yes,' Lucinda confessed.

Lady Hastings smiled.

'It is very tiring travelling. Now, I have dispatched a letter to your guardian's house in town first thing this morning.'

Mr Ferris was, of course, her guardian and was therefore due loyalty and obedience. Yet she hoped she would see the handsome captain again.

* * *

It had been a dismal morning for manoeuvres. Back at his sparse but adequate quarters with their rain-grey walls, Private Gardiner was hopping about from one foot to the other. A glutton for punishment, Robert knew his groom was impatient to take his boots for another merciless polishing.

'You're late back, Cap'n, Mon-sew, sir.'

'Well observed.'

Robert found he was in an uncharacteristically bad temper. Was he starting to tire of army life? It had been different out in the Peninsula. You had to be alert every minute of the day, just in case danger was waiting around the corner. A searing pain shot up his arm as a timely reminder. He may have learned that lesson just a bit too late, to his cost, but it was better than kicking his heels in Hounslow.

The picture of Miss Lucinda Handscombe sprang into his mind. Her form rose like a spectre, berating him for his indifferent treatment of her yesterday! Well, what did she expect? She was a school-chit, not a duchess, and she had caused him the most dreadful inconvenience. Her eyes had flashed like pools of ink but then he remembered her smile and the way it made her left cheek dimple.

At Lady Hastings' house, the ladies were sat in the drawing-room, when Lucinda heard the unmistakable crunching sound of a coach arriving on the gravel outside.

'Ah,' Lady Hastings exclaimed, 'it is unusually early for visiting. I'll warrant that is your guardian, Mr Ferris.'

He was shown directly into the drawing-room.

'Lucinda!'

His voice shook with relief.

'I came here directly when I received Lady Hastings' note. It is most fortunate that you are safe and well. I do not understand how we lost you!'

Lady Hastings stood up to face him.

'Good day, madam! I thank you sincerely for taking care of my ward. Let me send you some fine Canary wine, a small token of my gratitude. Come, Lucinda. We must be on our way.'

Lady Hastings' expression was as black as thunder.

'It is fortunate that Miss Handscombe found her way into the care of someone responsible.'

'Responsible?' Mr Ferris's eyes widened. 'I will have you know that I imagined Lucinda utterly ruined, snatched from under my nose, as she was, by a despicable rogue, masquerading as a dragoon.'

Despicable rogue! Lucinda bit her tongue. The captain was a gentleman and if it had not been for his kindness, goodness knows what could have happened.

'There have clearly been some misunderstandings which will no doubt be revealed in time,' Lady Hastings said, 'but in the meantime, I demand a full explanation of your own conduct before I release Miss Handscombe back into your guardianship!'

'What?' Mr Ferris stammered as he took a step backwards.

'Miss Handscombe, it might be better

if your guardian and I had this discussion alone. Perhaps you would care to investigate my library. I am sure you will find something that interests you.'

Lucinda rose and fled as quickly as she could. By the mahogany grandfather clock it was thankfully only a few minutes before she was summoned back. Lady Hastings was looking dignified while Mr Ferris looked puffed up with stifled vexation. Oh, dear!

'Miss Handscombe, I am delighted to say that your guardian has agreed that you may stay here for a few days while he conducts some urgent business in town. I would be very happy to have you as my guest.'

'Thank you, Lady Hastings,' Lucinda said before turning to face her guardian. 'Is not your sister in Richmond expecting us?'

'She is indisposed.' Mr Ferris coughed.

'Oh, dear. Please send her my good wishes and let her know that I look forward to making her acquaintance when she is recovered.'

Lady Hastings rustled her skirts as she adjusted her seat.

'Mr Ferris, I know you will know that I only have your ward's best interests at heart as I touch on this delicate subject, but Miss Handscombe has a requirement for a few items of clothing, a few dresses and such.'

Mr Ferris's face blanched and then coloured scarlet. If he was about to protest, he thought the better of it.

'I know a very talented mantua-maker. As I am one of her most important customers, I am sure she will be very obliging.'

Mr Ferris swallowed and raised his eyebrows.

'Madam, I defer to your higher judgment.'

'That is settled then.' Lady Hastings smiled.

Mr Ferris pushed his shoulders back so that he stood up straighter.

'Lady Hastings, I wonder if you would be so good as to allow me a moment alone with Miss Handscombe.'

'Of course.' Lady Hastings nodded, and left them.

Mr Ferris sat down in the chair next to Lucinda's. His disposition now appeared remarkably calm. Was he about to say something of import?

'Miss Handscombe, I am not a man of many or fancy words, and therefore I simply ask you if you would do me the honour of giving me your hand in marriage.'

Lucinda stared at her guardian. Had she heard him quite correctly? It was so completely unexpected. She could not marry him, could she?

'Mr Ferris, I thank you for your kind proposal. I . . . '

What if she refused him now? Would he continue to honour his obligations as her guardian, or would she truly be alone again in the world? What if this man, whom she now came to think on as something of her own, were to desert her for good?

'Miss Handscombe, you would do me the greatest honour by consenting to be my wife. Your father would have approved.'

Dear Papa, Papa who lay at the bottom of the ocean. He must have considered Mr Ferris a suitable guardian therefore why not a suitable husband? Lucinda clasped her hands together tightly. The captain's words on Mr Ferris rang in her ears — he has the appearance of a man more in the guise of a lover.

A girl in her situation, without money or kin, did not have the luxury of casting aside a good prospect on a whim.

'Miss Handscombe?'

She turned towards him and caught his eye.

'Mr Ferris, I cannot accept your kind offer of marriage.'

The door was pushed open and Lady Hastings swept in.

'I am sorry if I have interrupted. The carriage is prepared. We go to the mantua-maker. Mr Ferris, I am so sorry that your visit must be curtailed. I am sure you understand the urgency of having your ward clothed properly.'

Mr Ferris stood up and gave a little bow.

'I, too, must be on my way. I trust she will enjoy a pleasant stay.'

'And then?'

'I have pressing business that necessitates a visit to the island of Madeira. We sail in three weeks.'

Sail? Something tore at Lucinda's chest. Her throat constricted. It was difficult to breathe and every breath was desperate to break into a sob.

'Sea voyage?' Lucinda found she was shaking.

'What on earth is the matter, child?' Lady Hastings said.

'I do not think I should like to travel on the sea.'

'My dear, sea travel can be made tolerably comfortably these days. I am sure Mr Ferris will do everything to ensure you have an agreeable voyage.'

Lucinda shut her eyes and opened them. Everything in the room looked distorted. She had clasped the corner of the satin cushion tightly in her left hand. Surely Mr Ferris knew her family history.

'I do not think it would suit. My mother, my father and my brother were all drowned at sea. I do not think it is quite the thing for my family.'

'Of course, m'dear,' Mr Ferris said, 'I quite understand. I am sorry that I did not have the foresight to warn you we must go to Madeira. You will find that by facing the fear, it will evaporate. There is no need to be distressed.'

Mr Ferris seized her right hand and kissed it! Lucinda suppressed the urge to snatch her hand back again as if it had been scalded. She liked Ferris tolerably enough, as her guardian, but as her husband? Most certainly not! She forced herself to smile.

'I am much obliged, sir.'

He smiled at her as if he had got what he wanted. Let him think that if he chose. She would be dutiful to her guardian. She was grateful that he realised his obligations, however late, but if he thought he would be able to force her to sail on a ship she would defy him.

★　★　★

Robert stretched himself out as best he could. Whoever had furnished the barracks had seen fit only to provide this room with a single stout wooden chair. A pile of papers lay on the desk needing attention and he was supposed to be writing a report. It could wait. If he was going to Brentford, he had better go now.

Ten minutes later, Robert swung himself up on to Armada and set off towards Brentford at breakneck pace. In truth, he did not have time for this visit, but he had a duty to call on Lady Hastings and discover if the young miss had been reunited with her guardian after all.

He was shown directly into the

drawing-room where the two ladies sat.

'Lady Hastings, Miss Handscombe.' He nodded and tried to ignore a confounded odd feeling of light-headedness. 'Your servant.'

Miss Handscombe was still here! Why had her guardian not removed her already? The obviously borrowed dress did not fit her exactly but it was a vast improvement on the dismal garments she had been wearing before. Her hair had been arranged nicely. She had scrubbed up well.

'Robert, what a pleasure to see you again so soon,' Lady Hastings said.

'Good morning, Captain Monceaux.'

Miss Handscombe's bright eyes framed with their feathery lashes showed a certain compelling contentment.

'I am sorry for the lateness of my visit. My duties prevented me from calling yesterday.'

'We are delighted to see you at any hour, are we not?'

The dimple appeared on Miss Handscombe's cheek. She cast a glance at Lady Hastings before turning her eyes back on him.

'Of course! Now, Robert, would you like some refreshment? We have just had some tea but perhaps wine would be more the thing.'

Robert accepted a small glass of wine thankfully. He chose a chair opposite the ladies and took a small sip of his wine.

'I trust that Miss Handscombe is fully recovered?'

'Is it not apparent that I am quite recovered, sir, although I thank you for your kind enquiry.'

'Yes, I see I have no fear to worry that you would be permanently overset.'

'You will be relieved to hear that Miss Handscombe has been reunited with her guardian,' Lady Hastings announced.

'I am very pleased for Miss Handscombe,' he replied yet something akin to disappointment washed through him.

'Oh, yes, I am sure Mr Ferris would

want to thank you greatly and I, too, Captain Monceaux, for I confess that I am not sure I thanked you properly before,' Lucinda said.

'You thanked me quite adequately, Miss Handscombe.'

Robert marvelled at the coolness of his tone, but was it really necessary for him to sound quite so pompous?

'Mr Ferris has returned to London on business,' Lady Hastings clarified, 'but Miss Handscombe has kindly agreed to stay with me for a week or two as my guest. Well, I hope she will be still with me for the Phillips's ball.'

Miss Handscombe was to be in Brentford for a week, maybe two. The moment of that good news deserved savouring with a long sip of the very good wine. It was as if he had just been granted a stay of execution.

'At least a week? I hope you will make the most of it, Miss Handscombe, for Brentford and the surrounding neighbourhood hold many delights.'

He was speaking too quickly and

carelessly. He must impose some sort of order on his jumbled thoughts.

'Perhaps, Miss Handscombe,' he said, 'I might call on you again, and if the weather is not too inclement we might enjoy a ride.'

Robert knew he sounded calm, but in his chest his heart was now racing in anticipation of her reaction.

'I am afraid, Robert,' Lady Hastings replied, 'that it would not be appropriate. Miss Handscombe leaves for Madeira with her guardian in three weeks. They have an understanding.'

'Congratulations on your forthcoming nuptials,' he heard himself saying.

He excused himself, but it was not until he was out of the house and into the cold night that the truth hit him hard. He had been wounded because he had wanted her. There was nothing to be done except undertake a concerted campaign to banish every thought of her.

4

Lady Hastings had eight guests to dine that evening. The first course was a white soup, which Lucinda found quite easy to manage. The difficulty lay in keeping up with the fast-moving conversation around the table. Then something Mr Denton, a surveyor, said caught her attention and Lucinda found she was speaking to the company for the first time.

'You mean it is possible to travel all the way from London to Buckingham-shire by water?'

'Yes, Miss Handscombe.' Mr Denton's eyes flashed brightly. 'A piece of coal or yard of linen might complete the journey with relative ease, but not a young lady.'

'There is the Paddington Packet which takes fare-paying passengers from Uxbridge to Paddington in London,'

Lady Hastings said.

Lucinda was not interested in the Paddington Packet. She found her mind wandering back to Mr Denton's statement that it was now possible to travel by canal to Buckinghamshire. Her friend, Catherine, lived in Buckinghamshire . . .

* * *

'We've found her!' Cunningham was slightly out of breath. 'She is staying with a certain Lady Hastings in Brentford, and the man who rescued her is Captain Robert Monceaux. We intercepted a note.'

Cunningham shuffled through the bunch of papers in his hand.

'His father was George John Robert Monceaux, now deceased.'

'Is he rich, or poor as a church mouse?' Lord Rawleigh demanded.

'There are about two thousand acres in Ireland which are tenant farmed. He is a captain in the Fifteenth King's Dragoons. The regiment is stationed at

Hounslow having just lately returned from Portugal. The captaincy was purchased by commission in 1808 and may have been part financed by a bill signed by the Duke of Stanbridge.'

'Stanbridge?' the gentleman muttered to himself.

It was a name he recognised. Stanbridge was a wealthy landowner. Although it appeared that the dragoon had innocently rescued the chit from the highway robbery, it was still a setback. Ferris could be dealt with easily. He was only a wine merchant, but if the dragoon's connection to Stanbridge was proved, he could certainly be a more difficult prospect.

'I need a way in. I want a list of Lady Hastings' friends and connections. Come back to me tomorrow afternoon, or sooner if you discover something.'

* * *

'This evening is going to be a success, I am sure,' Lady Hastings said one morning at breakfast.

Lucinda could hardly believe she had been in Brentford a week.

'I've never been to a soirée before.'

'Now, Lucinda, it is really nothing to be anxious about. If you are unsure of what to say, just smile and remark on how happy you are to be staying in Brentford, and how fortunate we are, into winter, to have not yet had snow.'

'I shall remember that, Lady Hastings, thank you.'

'We have over three dozen attending and I had a note yesterday from Lord Tredorick asking if he might bring his guest, Lord Rawleigh. I do not know the man but there is every chance he is single and of good fortune.'

Lady Hastings had been pointing single men of fortune out to her all week, Lucinda thought. The captain would make someone a fine husband but Lady Hastings seemed to have disregarded him.

'Lady Hastings, you informed Captain Monceaux that I had an

understanding with my guardian.'

'Ah! I see your reasoning, dear child. We must correct that error lest dear Robert gives that impression to others. Do not worry. I shall speak to him.'

'I do not understand why you told him in the first place, Lady Hastings.'

'I wanted to ensure that Robert did not begin to have any ideas as towards your person. Robert is kind, honourable and of good family but he hasn't got a penny. He would be hard pressed to afford a wife.'

That evening, Lucinda wore one of her new dresses, mauve silk trimmed with sarsnet, and stayed alongside Lady Hastings in the drawing-room. She had made the acquaintance of a number in local Society and was reassured to see a few familiar faces arrive.

'Miss Handscombe?'

'Good evening, Mr Denton.'

'Now, I hope your interest in the canals was not feigned, for young ladies are wont to do such things. I have most especially brought you a chart which illustrates the routes of the canals all the way from London to Northamptonshire.'

Lucinda's annoyance at the first part of his remark was quashed by her delight at the map. Mr Denton's chart would prove if the half-baked plan she had formed was possible.

'Mr Denton, you are too kind!'

When she looked up from tucking the map away in her reticule she found Lady Hastings and Mr Denton had both gone and she was alone. She looked around the tableaux of faces in the drawing-room but did not see any she recognised.

A gentleman with raven dark looks and hooded eyes came upon her.

'Your servant, ma'am,' he said.

'Good evening, sir.'

Lucinda was surprised at the evenness of her voice. She sounded quite the accomplished lady and it seemed easy to add boldly, 'Forgive me, but I do not believe we have been introduced.'

'Let me correct that oversight,' the

gentleman replied, his cultured voice smooth as butter. 'I am Adam Charlesworth, Lord Rawleigh.'

'Miss Handscombe.'

'Ah, Lady Hastings' guest. What an unexpected pleasure. I trust that you are enjoying your stay?'

'Yes, of course. Brentford is delightful.'

He was watching her intensely, making Lucinda rather ill-at-ease.

'Then you cannot yet have been to town,' he said quickly. 'Middlesex is pleasant enough but I cannot think of anyone visiting other than as a staging post on the way to London.'

'How true, sir,' she replied, 'for I am a visitor bound for London myself.'

'In which part of town are your relations?' Lord Rawleigh enquired with a nonchalant air that Lucinda found suddenly unconvincing.

He was clearly no fool. She was being questioned about her background, and as soon as her lack of it was revealed, this handsome lord would go to ground.

'My guardian lives in London.'

'Is he here this evening?'

'No.'

'How delightful!' He smiled. 'We may have the opportunity to get to know one another a little better after all. There is nothing like a watchful guardian to spoil a perfectly good friendship between a lady and a man.'

Lucinda found herself feeling a little alarmed and then chided herself. What could happen within the confines of Lady Hastings' drawing-room?

He tilted his head slightly.

'I have a notion that beneath those pretty curls is a woman of some substance I should like to get to know better.'

This was absurd flattery. Lord Rawleigh was obviously a rake, and accustomed to flirtation, Lucinda decided, and she would be pleased to see him move on and cast his attentions towards some other female.

Robert stiffened as he stepped into Lady Hastings' drawing-room. He saw her at once. The pale dress flared over the curve of her hips before cascading straight to the ground. A stray strand of her hair had unfastened itself, and it curled over the right side of her forehead, Robert noticed to his annoyance. What was it about the chit that forced him to consider every single detail of her? Robert turned to Major Byrne, his companion.

'You see the couple conversing over there? He is Lord Rawleigh. I met him very recently. What do you know of him?'

'All of London knows Lord Rawleigh is a notorious gambler,' the major said with a smile. 'He is said to be on the verge of ruin.'

A gambler on the verge of ruin! Robert kept his voice even.

'And the lady, Miss Handscombe?'

'Never heard of her.' Byrne chuckled. 'The best thing for Rawleigh would be if he could catch an heiress, but who in their right mind is going to let him near their daughter? I might take it on myself to warn the girl or her family if I were you, Monceaux. I know it's not done to queer the pitch for another fellow but not everyone is privy to the latest London gossip and some of these country lasses are frightfully naïve.'

Robert nodded and strode directly towards them.

'Good evening, Miss Handscombe.'

'Good evening, Captain Monceaux,' Lucinda said as elegantly as she could. 'Are you acquainted with Lord Rawleigh?'

There was an unmistakable glint of danger in the captain's eyes. Lucinda felt her heart start to beat slightly faster.

'No. Captain Robert Monceaux of the Fifteenth Light Dragoons.'

'Lord Rawleigh,' the haughty reply came.

'We are so fortunate,' Lucinda said, 'for it to be so far into winter and as yet no snow.'

'Yes, very fortunate,' Rawleigh drawled. 'Indeed.'

The captain paused, his expression

appeared unnaturally cool. Then he turned to her, his countenance unchanged.

'It has been so pleasant renewing our acquaintance, Miss Handscombe. I trust the remainder of your stay with Lady Hastings will pass to your satisfaction.'

'Yes, thank you.'

Then he turned on his heel and walked away, right out of the room. How vexing! He had been so kind to her. She must never forget that he had gone out of his way to help her and that it was he who had brought her to Lady Hastings. Lucinda hoped later, when Lord Rawleigh left her alone, she would have another opportunity to converse with the captain.

'Mmmm,' Lord Rawleigh said, brushing her elbow in a most unexpected fashion as he reached to take her glass. 'I wonder if I might fill your glass, Miss Handscombe.'

'Oh! I should very much like another lemonade,' Lucinda replied quickly.

She really was starting to dislike Lord

Rawleigh and her instinct was not to trust him. As soon as he had gone, Lucinda hurried over to Lady Hastings' side and followed her when she had finished her conversation through to the morning-room, and the captain!

His dolman jacket sat on his broad shoulders more perfectly than any other man's. Tucked around his throat was a silk cravat. Lucinda was fascinated in how it pushed against the beginnings of bristle of his clean-shaven chin. He looked quite splendid. She nodded her head slightly and wished that her heart would slow down a little.

'If you will excuse me a moment,' Lady Hastings said and left them.

'I trust you are quite well.'

His pleasant, velvet voice melted her heart and his brown eyes held her gaze. She could not look away. She did not want to look away. What happy chance had brought them this moment together, in such a crowd?

'I am quite well, thank you. I trust you are well, sir, and Armada?'

The captain laughed.

'She is a fine horse, and quite in sorts. Shall I pass on your good wishes?'

'I should be obliged if you did,' Lucinda replied, smiling. 'May I ask how she came by her name?'

'She is fearless, if somewhat blown by the wind. There is also a story that somewhere in the Monceaux family past is some Spanish blood, from a pirate, shipwrecked it is said from the Armada in Irish soil. How true or not it is no-one seems to know for sure.'

His silky burr was, of course, Irish! How had she managed not to identify it before?

'Where in Ireland is your family from?' Lucinda asked.

'County Wicklow.'

'Have you been with your regiment abroad?'

'Yes.' His jaw clenched. 'I have been in Portugal.'

The memory must be troubling him, so much so that he had difficulty returning to his blithe demeanour of a moment ago. What was the cause of his distress? Had he been in the wretched retreat to Corunna this time last year? She had heard it had been a race to get their soldiers evacuated on to the ships before it ended in a massacre.

Should she share some of her own burdens? She certainly owed him after his kindness to her.

'Speaking of shipwrecks,' she said, 'my parents and brother were all drowned in a shipwreck in the West Indies. I have a great inclination to travel, but I am left with very little desire to undertake a sea voyage myself.'

'One day, you shall sail on a ship.'

He seemed to have an air of confidence in his voice. Lucinda felt a haze descend over her eyes. She was hardly sure she could see properly, or think. She would never go on a ship, ever. She heard the captain clear his throat, yet somehow the fragile intimacy they had built up over the last few minutes had shattered. What could she say to him?

'Ah, Miss Handscombe, your lemonade.'

Lord Rawleigh's hooded gaze was the last thing she wanted. He was close, too close. Lucinda did not approve of female trickery but when the alternative was Lord Rawleigh inching ever closer . . . She slumped to the floor. It was to be hoped that, on her début, she was a convincing actress.

'Miss Handscombe! Has she fainted?' the shrill voice of a lady came.

A number of people were moving towards her.

'Oh, dear, where are my smelling salts?'

Lady Hastings was practical, as ever. Someone tucked a cushion under Lucinda's shoulders. Someone was leaning over her so intimately she could smell him, feel his breath on her cheek. Even without opening her eyes, she knew it was the captain. Now she might really faint!

5

Lucinda couldn't breathe. Her eyes shot open. Lady Hastings had found her smelling salts! Her eyes stung and watered, and she could not see clearly.

'Robert, will you take Lucinda upstairs?' Lady Hastings clear voice cut through the murmurings.

The captain scooped her up as if she was as light as a feather. She let her head loll against his strong forearms, feeling secure, protected. She hardly noticed him mounting the stairs.

'In here,' Lady Hastings said.

From the corner of her eye she saw it was her bedroom. To think that the captain had entered her chamber! He laid her gently on her bed and all too quickly he had moved away. Lucinda flickered her eyes open. He was standing facing Lady Hastings by the door, his back to her.

'Thank you, Robert. I can always rely on you,' Lady Hastings said.

'It is nothing,' he replied, his voice husky and soft.

He would go back downstairs now, to the guests. The moment had passed. At least she had been saved from Lord Rawleigh.

'Thank you,' she whispered.

The captain turned and looked at her, his eyes disturbed. They widened as he caught her gaze. He was now regarding her with undisguised concern. As she blinked, he looked away, swallowing. He nodded and left the room abruptly. She heard his footsteps get farther and farther away.

Was she losing all her senses in this feeling she had for the captain? It was not every day that a girl was carried upstairs to her chamber by a cavalry officer in regimentals.

'I shall send up Mary,' Lady Hastings said.

'Yes, I think I had better retire.'

Later, when the other guests had all

departed, Robert followed Lady Hastings at her behest into the library. He poured two glasses of wine at Lady Hastings' request.

'It is not surprising that she was somewhat overset. Mr Ferris is coming on Monday to take her to Madeira. She does not wish to go, the dear child, and no doubt she will end up marrying him.'

Robert could see Lady Hastings was uneasy.

'It is most singular that he has only tried to visit the girl once this week!'

'I understand your sentiments with regards to Mr Ferris.'

Robert felt his jaw tighten.

'He does supply the Royal household,' Lady Hastings said.

'Confound the Royal household! Since when did that qualify a man to be a suitable guardian, or husband even?' Robert interrupted savagely.

'You are right, dear Robert. I was wondering if perhaps something might come of Lord Rawleigh's interest, but we have so little time.'

'Lord Rawleigh?' Robert tried to swallow his intense irritation. 'He would be a most unsuitable husband! He is a gambler and up to his ears in debt.'

'Oh? I was not aware. Such a charming young man, though.'

'I do not suppose he would be interested in marrying without money.'

'I have said she may stay with me as long as she likes, but I fear she feels that she would be an imposition. It would have been most satisfactory to have been able to secure her a husband. The poor girl is adrift.'

Robert jolted. Lady Hastings was looking at him with an expectant gaze.

'If there is anything I can do.'

Now, why had he said that?

'Yes, Robert! Have I been blind all this time? But surely you could not afford to keep a wife.'

He could not deny it did not appeal, at least in one sense, but that was a hundred miles from the reality of here and now. Robert cleared his throat.

'No, you are correct, I cannot afford . . . '

'Now, I have been thinking that if it was necessary I have the funds to provide Lucinda with a modest portion. Dear Robert, your dear mother would be so happy, too, to see you settled.'

'Marriage? I had not considered that. Surely we might discover some better solution.'

'Perhaps you are right. Why do you not come on Sunday, before we go to church, and speak with her? She admires you and will listen to your counsel. Try to dissuade her from going with Mr Ferris to Madeira.'

Robert felt his breath draw up short. Was it too much to hope that Miss Handscombe might have developed some feelings towards him? Nonsense! If she admired him it was the admiration that any young lady would naturally have for a gentleman in regimental uniform.

Lady Hastings was looking at him expectantly.

'Assuming Miss Handscombe has no objection, I will be happy to talk to her and try to discover what we might do best to assist her.'

★   ★   ★

Water, water was everywhere. Lucinda's mouth was dry and tasted of muslin. She tried to breathe evenly. It was deep, the sea, as deep as falling from a high cliff.

The waves pounded the ship like rain lashes against a house in a storm. She wanted to escape.

'Help! Help me!'

She recognised that voice! It was her own. She was awake! Lucinda opened her eyes and pushed herself to sit up. It was the middle of the night but the familiar order of her bedroom loomed in the moonlight. She gulped.

What a fantastical dream! She had never been at sea, nor did she ever intend to go. There was no necessity to travel by sea. Most people never left England, only sailors and soldiers, diplomats, and wine merchants!

Lucinda shivered and picked the matted strands of hair from her damp forehead. She slid back under the covers. Mr Ferris had sent a note yesterday saying they were to depart for Falmouth next Monday. Tomorrow was Thursday. She was running out of time.

The following morning, Lucinda stared at the vast arrangement of deep pink roses on the hall table made all the more spectacular bathed as they were in the shafts of winter sunshine.

'Roses in January!'

'Hothouse. They came for you,' Lady Hastings informed her as she swept into the hall.

'For me? Who on earth would have sent me flowers?'

'They are from Lord Rawleigh.'

'Oh.' Why was Lord Rawleigh sending her flowers? 'Is it customary to be sent flowers from, well, I don't know . . . ' Lucinda faltered.

'They came with a note,' Lady Hastings said, gesturing to a silver plate on the sideboard.

A sliver of paper lay there, indeed addressed to her. Lucinda broke the seal and pulled the single sheet open.

'Lord Rawleigh sends his compliments.'

'We must try to discover his intentions,' Lady Hastings said.

'Do you think it is possible that Lord Rawleigh wants to marry me?'

'All I would say is that we should be aware of the possibility and therefore, as we know very little about the gentleman, I shall make some enquiries.'

'But I am to go to Madeira with Mr Ferris.'

'You certainly can go to Madeira with Mr Ferris if you so choose, but I thought you would have preferred not to have to go.'

'Mr Ferris is my guardian.'

'I do not see him come to visit his ward. When are you one and twenty?'

'Not for six months. My birthday is in June.'

'That is most unfortunate.'

Lady Hastings appeared about to continue, and then paused, as if she was trying to find the right words.

'Mr Ferris, you know, is not quite a gentleman.'

Lucinda had never considered it before but she knew that Lady Hastings was right. Mr Ferris was a man of means, but not a gentleman because he made his living from trade. Lord Rawleigh was every inch a gentleman, but also, even if nothing else, a rake.

Lucinda tried to keep her tone light.

'Lord Rawleigh appears to be a rake. I am caught between the devil and the deep blue sea.'

Lady Hastings chuckled. 'Not quite yet, m'dear. Most young bucks appear somewhat rakish. Lord Rawleigh will most likely turn out to be entirely respectable.'

* * *

'I do not like that word,' Rawleigh said, drumming fingers on the table.

The panes of both windows in his study rattled as a branch whipped them repeatedly.

'Abduction, then?' Cunningham suggested.

'I do not like that word either.'

'Rescue?'

'Rescue is better, for she surely cannot really wish to marry Ferris, when there is a peer of the realm after her hand.' Rawleigh gave a shaky laugh and puffed out his chest. 'I find myself already impatient with this courtship game. Time enough to court the chit after I have my ring on her finger. I shall feel a whole lot easier once my debts are cleared. Let us tarry no longer and set up something for Sunday. You can surely discover the church they attend and the time. 'Twill be easy. And find Ferris, will you? I don't want any trouble from that quarter. I am sure he will agree to be paid off.'

* * *

It was still early. Lucinda stared at herself in the glass and trembled. Sunday. It had taken an hour to arrange her hair. It was drawn up and back now, secured firmly with uncomfortable pins and combs, and at the back, perfect corkscrew curls cascaded down. Now her chest felt uncomfortably tight and her thoughts could not be torn away from the fact that tomorrow Mr Ferris was to visit.

There was a gentle knock at the door, and Lucinda knew from the manner it was Lady Hastings.

'We are a little early yet,' Lady Hastings said, 'but if you are ready, there is breakfast downstairs.'

Lucinda nodded, and found herself saying quickly, as she gathered up her skirts, 'Oh, yes, I will go now. There is nothing else to be done here.'

The thought of eating anything was far from her mind, but anything to distract her from the prospect of tomorrow was welcome.

'I will join you very shortly,' Lady Hastings replied. 'I just have one or two things to attend to before we go.'

Lucinda descended the stairs, but the hall was empty. She walked through the hall into the dining-room. The breakfast had been laid out on the buffet as usual. Lucinda lifted the lids of two of the platters. She stared out of the window as a crunching sound alerted her to the carriage being prepared for their imminent departure. Very soon they would be leaving to go to church.

She helped herself to a few dishes and sat down. Determined to do as any sensible girl ought, she took a bite, but her throat was as dry as a bone, and the ham felt as if it were a pebble of pumice. A jug of lemonade had been provided. Lucinda poured a small measure into a glass and drank it, and, briefly refreshed, she had the sudden fancy to go to the library.

It was her favourite place in the house. When she had wanted to be alone it had been the solitude of the library that she had sought. She would be able to think there, think what she should do. Lucinda pushed the door open and stepped inside, closing it carefully behind her.

'Good morning, Miss Handscombe.'

Lucinda started. What was the captain doing here?

He was standing in front of the heavy oak desk, looking as if he had been perusing the newspapers. Lucinda's mouth felt dry again. It was hot in here. The fire must have been going all morning and someone had recently stoked it.

'Miss Handscombe, you look unwell! Are you all right?'

'It is slightly too warm in here, perhaps.'

'Come, sit down.'

The captain walked around the desk and, brushing her elbow with his hand, guided her to the chair farthest from the fire. His touch like a searing heat, made her quiver.

'Would you like something to drink?' he inquired.

'Yes, please. Might I have a lemonade? There is a jug next door.'

He was back too quickly, with the jug of lemonade and two clean glasses. He placed them down on the table and went to open the window. A gust of cold air swept in. It stung Lucinda's face, but tasted delicious.

Lucinda watched the captain pour two glasses of lemonade. She forced her mind to focus on the lemonade and nothing else. It would be cool and refreshing. He handed her a glass, and as he did so, their fingers brushed. A brief touch, light as a feather, but it sent something through Lucinda as powerful and unlikely as a bolt of lightning.

Her hand was incapable of holding the glass and it crashed to the floor. Lemonade splashed across her dress, over the captain, and the floor.

Lucinda shrieked, jumping up, her heart pounding.

6

It did not smash,' Robert said immediately, paying no attention to the damp patches across his breeches. He bent to pick up the glass.

She would rather that he had scolded her! His gentle manner was just not the thing at all. Lucinda sank back into her chair and began to sob.

'A little lemonade spilled, that is all it is,' he said and pushed a white linen handkerchief into her hands. 'There is no need to overset yourself,' she heard him say in a caring manner. 'Tell me what is the matter and I am sure we will find a simple remedy.'

'I do not wish to go to Madeira.'

'You do not have to do anything you choose not to.'

'Mr Ferris wishes me to go to Madeira. It behoves me to obey him. Moreover,' she continued, 'I have nowhere else to go. If I do not agree, I shall be forced to earn my own living as little better than a servant as a teacher or governess, or I might be so lucky to come by a position as a companion. Lady Hastings has, out of pity, offered me such a position already.'

She stopped. He was on his knees before her, clasping her bare hands in his own. Then his brown eyes moved in towards her. His lips met hers, then came immediate darkness. The chair creaked as she leaned backwards. His hands captured her, his fingers cradled her chin. Her thoughts became disturbed. His warm mouth captured hers. There was force and vigour behind the unyielding softness.

She would have stumbled had she been standing. Her knees had buckled, and then came the shock that she was not shocked. She should be! She felt the velvet touch of his hands cupping her face, the heady demands of his mouth upon hers and the invitation to respond. Then he pulled away as surely as if she had slapped him.

Robert scrambled to his feet. What in heaven's name had possessed him? He knew full well and was not pleased. No gentleman allowed his baser instincts to rule him. He had ceased to see anything except her small, round face, and the challenge of her sad blue eyes.

He pulled his jacket straight and dusted off his cuffs. Just as she had stirred his protective instincts before, she had woken them again now. Dusting off his knees could wait. Right now it seemed better to keep standing straight, in a manly fashion. He realised she had never been kissed before, yet she was looking at him as if what she actually wanted was to be kissed again!

She had to know that it wasn't going to happen again, and he must apologise. He looked at her and her expression changed. Her mouth fell. She paled, and began to shake. He would have cursed himself, if it had done any good, and fully intended that next moment to offer his apology, but she leaped from the chair and pushed past him. He turned and flew straight after her, but she was too quick. As he arrived at the foot of the stairs, she had already reached the top. She disappeared out of sight, and the thud of a door told him that she was safe in her chamber.

The commotion drew Lady Hastings and her maid on to the landing. Robert bounded up the stairs, to meet Lady Hastings' questioning gaze.

'I'm afraid that Miss Handscombe is rather upset.'

Lady Hastings did not deflect from looking at him.

'Oh, dear,' she responded.

'She does not wish to go to Madeira,' he explained.

'I fear that will be a most indelicate and difficult situation with her guardian,' Lady Hastings replied.

'Well, what is to be done?'

'Yes, what is to be done?' Lady Hastings echoed. 'Let me first be sure in my own mind what the child really does want. Wait downstairs, Robert, for I will no doubt be obliged shortly for your help.'

Robert nodded and made his way downstairs, and without thinking, returned to the library. He had certainly not assisted her as he had promised, but simply caused her all the more misery. He must learn to temper his impetuous nature. Confound it! She might have been suffering nerves, but his inappropriate actions could only have strengthened any apprehensions she might be harbouring.

The library door opened to reveal Lady Hastings.

'It seems you are right. Lucinda says she does not want to go to Madeira. I suppose there is nothing for it but to offer her a home here for the foreseeable future. Now, I really must go to church or there will be such a to-do. I have not missed a Sunday service in thirty years. Lucinda, however, may be indisposed. Will you stay here, Robert, in case Mr Ferris decides to arrive a day early? Nearly all the servants have gone to church already. He might choose to return here.'

Robert saw Lady Hastings out to the carriage. Then, shutting the heavy front door, Robert turned to look at the staircase with an agony of indecision. Something in him wanted to go to Lucinda, and yet there was perhaps a better judgment that advised him to retire to the library to wait. For what? To wait for Ferris to come and cart off his ward?

This situation, he could not forget, was at least in part his own making, and he should do something to try and affect the best outcome. By her own admission, Miss Handscombe did not desire to become a governess or companion. The only option was marriage! She had no family to guide and protect her and no portion to attract a husband. It would be an act of charity worthy of any true gentle-man to offer for her. Did he have the selflessness within him to do it?

The problem was, could he support a wife? He could resign his commission and return to Ireland, but would there be enough to support his wife and a family as well as his mother and three unmarried sisters?

Robert realised he had run through all the arguments and only one was compelling. If Ferris came and removed his ward, as he had every right to do, the man could no doubt force her to marry him, and she would have no-one to defend her. Lady Hastings might offer her a position, but she would not stand in Ferris's way. Robert knew he was in a position to offer her much more himself, the protection of his name. She would be his wife and beholden to Ferris no more.

Robert climbed the stairs cautiously, wondering at every step if he was doing the right thing, or should he turn back? He found her in a room that appeared to be a dressing-room. She sat frighteningly still on a low stool with her back to him. It looked as though she must be staring blindly out of the window that faced towards the gardens.

'Miss Handscombe?' he said softly.

She turned around. She had in fact been reading a piece of paper, which she still held in her hand. It looked like a map.

'Captain Monceaux, what on earth brings you here?'

Robert took a couple of steps nearer. At this closer distance, her pallor was arresting, although she had every appearance of calm.

'I came to enquire if you were all right, and . . . ' Robert faltered.

Now it came to it, it was hardly the easiest of things to say. He needed her to know that although this was a marriage of convenience, a genuine warmth lay behind his words. He would work at building some sort of life for them. He swallowed. The prospect of wedding her was hardly unappealing. In fact, it burned within him, like a flame that refused to be extinguished.

She was looking at him curiously, and

he had to say something.

'I wondered if you would like a glass of lemonade.'

'Thank you.'

'Perhaps we should return down-stairs. May I escort you?'

Those same lips that had crushed against hers were gently curved. It was a kind, polite smile that belied what she knew him capable of. Never had her opinion of a person been so wholly turned upside down. She had thought the captain kind and trustworthy. Now she knew he could be dangerous, as he had nearly made her lose all her sense and reason.

Most frightening had been the leap of excitement that had sprung up in her, and the terrible compulsion she had felt to kiss him back, with equal ardour. He had made it so that she could no longer even trust herself. Downstairs would be much safer than here, she thought.

She placed the plan of the canal on the dressing-table, making a note to remember she had left it there. She would need to come back to it later.

It felt easy enough to sit in the drawing-room and take the glass of lemonade he fetched for her. He had taken a seat next to hers.

'Miss Handscombe, your desire not to have to travel with your guardian to Madeira is quite understandable.'

Lucinda opened her mouth, but how could she explain about slimy sea monsters, large black waves and ship-wrecks? She was jolted back into consciousness by his sudden question.

'It is the most ill-suited of moments and yet perhaps the best. I do not know, but I wondered if I might be of some service to you by offering you the protection of my name.'

His eyes looked sincere. His brow had creased.

'Am I to understand, sir, that you are offering me marriage?'

There was no whirlwind in her mind, or happiness coursing through her veins. No fanfare of trumpets sounded.

All was quiet in Lady Hastings' drawing-room, save the ordinary crackle of the fire and the tick-tock from the clock on the mantelpiece.

'Yes,' he replied, and his expression said it all — pity!

Lucinda drew up her skirts, and, rustling, rose and walked over to the window. She had declined Mr Ferris's proposal and shuddered at the prospect of Lord Rawleigh's. Now, amazingly, she was being offered something she had dreamed she wanted — marriage to a handsome dragoon officer.

She turned. He was watching her every move from under those thick dark eyelashes. Lucinda drew in a sharp breath. It would be so easy to throw herself into his arms, into his protection. Was her fear of the sea so strong that she would let it rule her, and push her into the arms of a man only motivated by pity?

She could not let him sacrifice himself in this way! No, she did not want to be ruled by a fear, even if it gave her the captain. Besides, the captain had scared her by what he had shown her of herself. No man would stand for such passions in a wife. Oh, she was too confused. He had pushed her feelings from being something unsettling to something else to run away from. Even now, a part of her hoped he would kiss her again!

The best solution was to run away. She had thought about it, and now she was sure. She could not take what was offered, in a cold-blooded way, knowing this gentleman's motivation was one of charity.

She returned to her seat and did not waver from regarding him as closely as he regarded her. She could not read his expression now. It was different, but she had certainly seen pity there earlier.

'Can you support a wife?' she asked.

It was to be hoped that he would answer her honestly and then she could decline his offer gently, in the way that his kindness deserved.

'Not really,' Robert replied.

In truth, he was somewhat taken aback. Was she so cold that she now sought to measure his proposal on its material benefits? He would not have credited it. He thought he saw a flash of disappointment cross her face but perhaps he imagined it.

'In that case, Captain Monceaux, I thank you sincerely for your kindness, but I am afraid I cannot accept your offer.'

Robert felt the heat of a sudden anger rising up inside. He had a sudden compulsion to seize her and attempt to kiss the life out of her. Oh, she vexed him intolerably! So, he was not good enough for her. As if she could afford to be so choosy!

He was not going to stand here and be tormented by her serene eyes any longer. Robert bowed, and he hoped she saw the mockery in it.

'I wish you luck in finding a husband who better meets your satisfaction! Good day, Miss Handscombe.'

He took his leave, slamming the drawing-room door shut.

* * *

Spying his man at the church engaged busily in selling dissenting pamphlets, Cunningham sauntered over as if to buy one.

'It's off, guv,' the hushed information came.

'What?' Cunningham said tersely.

'She didn't come to church.'

'You sure?'

'The carriage came but with just the old lady, guv.'

No sooner had these words been spoken than Cunningham saw the door of the church open and a clergyman, followed by the congregation, began to spill out. He saw an elderly lady emerge but there was no sign of the girl. He breathed a sigh of relief. He had not been convinced that seizing her from outside the church in the view of half of Brentford had been the greatest idea. It saved him a bungled job.

Meanwhile, back at the house,

Lucinda paced up and down the drawing-room. Of all the foolish notions, to offer marriage when he could not even support a wife!

The sunshine filtered through the windows, its imprint growing longer and weaker. Should she have accepted the captain's proposal? No! How could he be happy to have a drain of a wife he could not afford? What she needed to decide was how she could run away, and where would she go?

Her worldly wealth, besides her clothes, was two guineas given to her by Mr Ferris, and three shillings and sixpence she had saved from her meagre school allowance. She had no jewellery or trinkets of any value. It was hardly going to get her far when the costs of inns and coaching were taken into consideration.

Lady Hastings would be happy to have her as a guest for a while longer but would Mr Ferris allow it? She could not see him allowing her to thwart his plans. Captain Monceaux kept coming back into her thoughts. She most certainly did not want to see him again. Every time, it seemed to get worse, being drawn into his gaze, the heat of his touch.

The idea of never seeing him again was sending tear pricks to her eyes but he could not support a wife and she could not have her heart broken by throwing herself at a husband who looked on her as charity.

There was only one solution. She must get away. She would have to earn her living as a teacher again. She would go to Catherine, a teacher herself and her dearest friend. She would help her. But how could she get to Catherine in Buckinghamshire for the princely sum of two guineas? It must be possible to go by canal, which avoided inns and coaching, and London altogether.

She found Mr Denton's map on her dressing-table. She spread it out on the writing-table in her bedroom and traced her finger through the places as the canal headed west, before starting to go north. Where was Wednesley, the village where Catherine lived?

She hastened downstairs to the library and found a book with a map of Buckinghamshire, and there she found Wednesley, not more than two or three miles from Harefield, a place on the canal plan! There was no time to lose. Mr Ferris came on the morrow.

7

Lucinda walked quickly along the road to New Brentford and the canal junction. She looked across the bustle of barges and people but could see no sight of a packet. All the boats seemed to have industrial cargo. How did a passenger get from here to Buckinghamshire?

She spied a woman carrying a pail of water. She thought she might ask her for assistance. The woman pointed to a barge across the way, where an older man sat, smoking his pipe, while a young lad attended to a tethered horse alongside. She hurried over to where the barge was moored.

'Do you take passengers, sir?'

The boatman peered blankly as she drew a guinea from her reticule.

'I am after a passage to Harefield, sir.'

The boatman's eyes fixed on the guinea and he nodded.

'Ain't my usual cargo, but I'll take you if you can dress less 'spicuous. Ain't no place for a lady.'

★ ★ ★

No sooner had Robert arrived back at the barracks, than Gardiner was at his door.

'I have here a letter for you, Cap'n Monceaux, sir.'

'Go on then,' Robert said. 'Who is the letter from?'

'Your old lady, er, Lady Monceaux, sir.'

His mother, Lady Monceaux, was his main correspondent and wrote about the meanest domestic subjects.

'Well, the letter, what is in it then?' Robert snapped.

'The Duke of Stan . . . ' Gardiner referred back to the document in his hands, his finger tracing the exact word. 'The Duke of Stanbridge.'

'The Duke of Stanbridge is my uncle, my mother's brother, although I have never actually met him,' Robert replied. 'I believe he is in Spain.'

'Was. He has passed away.'

Robert snatched the letter so he could read it for himself.

There was no doubt. He was now the Duke of Stanbridge, with vast responsibilities, his mother said! He was to resign his commission and go to see the lawyers in London immediately. As if he needed an excuse!

He had joined the army to find some purpose to his life, but surely these unexpected tidings were a better application. He had no intention of being, like his unfortunate uncle, a soldier and a duke. He'd never understood why with all his uncle's responsibilities at home, he'd decided to follow the drum.

He also knew exactly whom he wanted as the Duchess of Stanbridge! Now his circumstances were vastly improved, Lucinda was sure to accept him. She had refused him before, quite rightly, when he had admitted he could not support a wife. Her refusal had sounded wistful, as if she had allowed her reason to overrule her emotion. Given the opportunity, he would bombard her with passion and make her love him. Her response to his kiss had proved she was not insensible to him in that way.

He instructed Gardiner to have Armada saddled up. He could be in town before dark and hopefully do whatever business needed to be done. Tomorrow, he'd be back in Brentford to claim his bride . . .

But unknown to him, next dawn, Lucinda was already slipping out of the house, long before any of the servants were awake. The cold air pinched her face. It was black outside but the sky was clear of clouds.

Dressed in her oldest and most unflattering grey bombazine dress and with a woollen cloak, Lucinda was certain no-one would take her for a lady. She carried with her a small bundle of useful items, and her reticule and coin were tucked away safely.

She had not credited how eerie it felt walking through the deserted streets. She started to hurry. Even at the canal, there appeared to be no-one about. Where was her boatman? The spot where he had been moored yesterday was empty! Had they gone already? Was she too late? Then she heard a shout. There they were, over towards the bridge. The boatman was waving at her.

His horse, held by a boy, had already been hitched up to pull the barge. Lucinda grabbed her skirts and ran and was with them in a minute.

'I nearly missed you,' Lucinda said, slightly breathless.

He directed her to sit on a plank at the stern of the boat and then proceeded to ignore her. Only when Lucinda looked again to the horse and boy did she realise they were now moving. It was hardly possible to tell as the boat drifted lazily through the water.

Lady Hastings raced down the steps to meet Robert. From her look he knew that something was dreadfully wrong.

'Oh, Robert, I am so glad that you are here! She is gone!'

As if thrown into an ice-cold river, Robert felt his every sense slow down. It was today, wasn't it, that Ferris was due to come for her? He could not believe he had forgotten that!

'How can she have disappeared?'

'I think she may have been anxious that she must marry her guardian. I had a suspicion on that score.' Lady Hastings' voice sounded dull and tired. 'She must have run away.'

Robert was stunned. The short-lived sense of elation that she was not to marry Ferris made no impact on the feeling growing in his gut that he could only describe as emptiness.

'Did she truly have no family or friends?' he managed to say. 'What about her school?'

'Yes, I shall write to the seminary in Chippenham,' Lady Hastings said, brightening. 'It is always possible that she has gone there. Indeed, I did heard her mentioning a friend she wrote to.'

'The direction of this friend?' Robert demanded. 'The name?'

'I believe she did mention it.' Lady Hastings looked thoughtful. 'But I cannot remember.'

'I warrant she has either gone back to the school or to this friend,' Robert said without hesitation, trying to ignore the gripping fear that rather she may have been snatched against her will. 'There is no reason why she would not write to you shortly to let you know that she is safe and well.'

'I hope you are proved right. My mind is somewhat at rest at that thought.'

'I will send my man to all the post houses directly. If I can trace her, I will. You have my word. I will send any news as soon as I have it.'

* * *

Lucinda could tell from the sun that it was well past noon by the time they reached Harefield, where she was to disembark. It looked a large village and so it should be easy to find someone to transport her to Wednesley. If it came to it, she could always walk.

The relief at stepping down from the barge was shortlived. As Lucinda watched, the barge began to continue its slow, onward journey and she realised the grave potential danger she had placed herself in. She was alone and in an unknown part of the country. Highwaymen, as far as she knew, did not hold up canal vessels but now she was ashore, she needed to keep all her wits about her and hasten to Wednesley without delay.

A chestnut mare ridden by a tall gentleman stood silhouetted on a hillock overlooking the row of cottages by the canal. Armada? Robert? Lucinda's heart stuck in her throat, but the rider turned so she saw his face, a hard, unfamiliar face. Lucinda gulped. It was not the captain.

A woman from one of the cottages came hurrying over.

'Miss, can I be of help?'

Lucinda started.

'I wonder if you could help me. I need to find transport to the village of Wednesley.'

'I 'spect Jack, me husband, can take you. 'Tis not far.'

Lucinda's relief was immense, and soon she was aboard Jack's dogcart as it jolted along the unmade road to Wednesley.

What a pretty village it was. The church drew Lucinda's eye immediately it came into view with its mediaeval, tall square tower and imposing nave. Next to it was a neat row of tiled cottages and a smarter house, double-fronted, which must be the rectory. Lucinda looked at the church, the cottages and the rectory again. Had she been here before?

No, she could not remember ever having set foot in Buckinghamshire before. Was there somewhere else, very similar, of which she was thinking? There had been a village they had visited often when she had been very young. She could remember a house, brick, she was sure, red brick with white windows.

'I be lookin' for Miss Sinjon's 'ouse,' Jack said to a group of children.

The taller of the two boys whipped off his cap.

'Mister.' He nodded to Lucinda and added, 'Miss.'

Lucinda's eyes followed to where all five children pointed to the farthest away of the tiled cottages. Jack drove the cart right up to the cottage door. Lucinda stepped down. What if it transpired that Catherine had moved away? Lucinda forced herself to take a long, deep breath. She lifted her hand to the door and in answer to her tap, the door opened. Catherine!

'Lucy!' the girl exclaimed.

'Catherine! I am, I am . . . '

Lucinda looked to the waiting carter

and gave him his promised coin. Catherine bustled her friend into the hallway and through to the cottage's low-ceilinged sitting-room.

'I am sorry for my surprised expression. I had assumed when we next met it would be some years from now! You wrote to me saying that you were going to Madeira,' Catherine was saying.

'I am not going to Madeira. I have run away.'

Catherine clasped Lucinda's hands in her own as Lucinda explained as best as she could.

'You are quite right to run away,' Catherine said once Lucinda had finished her tale.

She had told Catherine the most of it, except for the captain. She had not mentioned him.

'I was not sure, but I could not bear to go to Madeira. Mr Ferris might have renewed his suit. He is an odious man.'

'You can stay here as long as you choose.'

'May I? Just until I find a position.'

'Lucy, you should marry! Do you not have a portion?'

'There was some money and that paid for my schooling but it ran out.' Lucinda sighed. 'For the last year, they kept me on out of kindness and I worked as a pupil teacher. It was a relief when Mr Ferris arrived because I do not know how much longer I could have stayed there.'

'Have you no idea if your father had a portion set aside for you somewhere, in a bank perhaps, or in bonds?'

'If any other funds existed, surely I would have known about it. My entire fortune stands at one guinea, two shillings and five pence.'

'Do you not have the details of your father's lawyers?'

'No.'

'I shall ask the parson, Mr Adams, for some advice for you.'

★ ★ ★

Robert was exhausted. Involuntarily, not trusting Gardiner to do the task adequately himself, they had been together to every posting house for miles. A drizzling mist had set in but they had continued along the Great West Road until they had visited every inn between Brentford and London and still they had found not a trace of her!

If her intention had been to disappear without trace she had succeeded. Eventually, he found an unfamiliar bed in an unfamiliar city. He had no wish to sleep but exhaustion must have finally overcome him . . .

★　★　★

'Stand and deliver!'

Lucinda woke up shaking, and blinked several times before she realised she was not in a darkened coach any more. She was in Catherine's cottage!

Lucinda shivered even though she was warm beneath the thick blankets and counterpane. She closed her eyes and across her mind it flashed again. The coach had come to a sudden halt, and the horses bolted. How? Someone must have cut their harnesses.

She opened her eyes again. The voice that had spoken the command was not one of a coarse ruffian but someone whose elocution was as clear as glass and whose voice was now familiar to her. But who was it now so clear in her memory?

8

Lucinda came downstairs just as Catherine came in through the back door with a jug of fresh milk.

'Catherine, I could not describe it exactly, but this place seemed strangely familiar to me when I arrived yesterday. I was wondering if I had perhaps been here before.'

'It might be possible,' Catherine said. 'I came by this post via the recommendation of your friend, Mrs Hodges. I think Mrs Hodges must have been in some way acquainted with the duke.'

'As far as I can remember, Mama only knew Mrs Hodges after we came to Bath, but I cannot fathom what connection Mrs Hodges might have had with a duke. Would it possible to ask the duke of it, do you think?'

Catherine frowned.

'The duke, I am afraid, is dead. He

died in the Peninsular. I only had the pleasure of making his acquaintance when I first arrived here.'

For just a moment there had been a duke who might have been acquainted with Mrs Hodges and might, just might have known something of her family. Now it was like the last piece of hope had just been smashed.

'There is a new duke, of course.' Catherine's expression brightened. 'He's the old duke's nephew, but he has not yet come here. It may be that he can help us. Come, let us breakfast, for I must shortly be to school.'

★ ★ ★

Lloyds was busy. A heavy mix of coffee and newsprint hit Robert as soon as he stepped in off the street. He'd only been in London since last evening and had got Rawleigh's note this morning. It was most decidedly not the usual place for gentlemen to meet. Did Rawleigh not have a club?

121

No matter, he was here. He had gone to Ferris's house earlier and his housekeeper had assured him that her guardian was gone to Madeira and, no, he did not have a lady of any description with him.

Robert chose an empty table in the middle of the room and sat facing the doors. Rawleigh was only a moment late. If Rawleigh had had some hand in Lucinda's disappearance, he would kill him.

Rawleigh spotted him at once and sat down opposite him.

'I think you know what this concerns.'

Robert did not like his expression, did not like the fact that he was sure something mysterious was going on.

'Miss Handscombe,' Rawleigh continued, 'and I are to be married. I am not at liberty to reveal her exact whereabouts. She is anxious to preserve her reputation.'

The confounded man may as well have taken a knife and driven it into

Robert's chest. It would have had the same effect.

'I would request that you desist in your active search for her as this will just draw further attention to her unwarranted absence. We are to be married in a few days.'

'So she never intended to marry her guardian?' Robert asked carefully.

'It is a slightly delicate situation with Miss Handscombe not yet one and twenty. Rest assured I have cleared things with Mr Ferris.'

No doubt you paid him handsomely for his consent, Robert thought.

'Why are you telling me this?' he asked.

'A natural concern for Lady Hastings. Miss Handscombe was frantic for me to somehow inform her that she was safe and well. I trust you would be so good as to pass on this news.'

This whole thing sounded far too flimsy. Rawleigh could have easily penned a note to Lady Hastings. There was a specific reason why he wanted this face-to-face meeting. He spoke once again.

'I wanted to make sure your feelings for Miss Handscombe ran to more than friendly concern. Miss Handscombe and I are desperately in love.'

'I don't believe it.'

Robert rose, pushing his chair back violently.

'Steady on, Stanbridge,' Rawleigh exclaimed but for the first time a small flicker of unease passed across his face.

'Steady on!' Robert laughed, deliberately loudly. 'I'll damn well call you out for besmirching a lady's honour.'

'No need to take it so badly, old fellow.'

'Name your seconds!' Robert growled.

Rawleigh leaped to his feet, a flash of panic in his eyes.

'I'll sell her to you.'

'What?'

'I will renège all claim on Miss Handscombe's person if you will deposit fifty thousand pounds with my bankers.'

Robert lightened his tone.

'Does that not assume that the lady in question is yours to sell?'

* * *

Catherine had insisted Lucinda write to Lady Hastings that very day. After three days, she received a reply and she was glad she had written and put the lady's mind at rest. But Lady Hastings' letter made no mention of the captain although it did mention that Mr Ferris had not called. Oh, dear, she was foolish thinking that the captain would bother to enquire about her, after she had so soundly refused him.

It snowed later that evening. Lucinda sat with Catherine in front of a roaring fire. She reached down for a piece of embroidery Catherine had persuaded her to start. There was a heavy knock at the door. Lucinda pricked her finger with the needle as Catherine got up to answer.

'Your Grace, please come in,' she

heard Catherine say.

It must be the duke — the new Duke of Stanbridge.

'Does my fame precede me already?'

The rich burr was tinged with a touch of amusement which made Lucinda start. Was the captain with him? Lucinda held her breath but only heard one voice. Lucinda sat as if frozen to her seat. Was it somehow possible that the captain and the new Duke of Stanbridge were one and the same?

She placed her needlework down, rose and turned to see the captain stepping into the sitting-room after Catherine.

'Robert Monceaux, your servant,' he said with a bow.

Catherine replied, 'Catherine St John. I look after the school in Wednesley, Your Grace.'

He turned to Lucinda, seemingly quite unperturbed.

'Delighted to make your acquaintance once again, Miss Handscombe.'

His eyes twinkled as if it was a great joke.

'Captain Monceaux.'

'Since we last met, though it was only a week ago, I have acquired a new title. Let me reintroduce myself as eighth Duke of Stanbridge.'

Lucinda made a little curtsey. How fast and unrelenting came her disappointment now. Captain Monceaux, her handsome dragoon and rescuer, was now a duke! How cruel were the fates that should transform her hero from a mere gentleman into an aristocrat and therefore remove him, for ever, from even her wildest dreams.

While she could dream that once in a while a cavalry officer might consent to marry a lady without family or fortune, it was inconceivable that a duke should do so.

Robert gave a formal bow and kissed her soft hand. She pulled it back sharply as if she had been branded. He caught her eye and held her gaze as long as he could until she shied and looked away.

Do not think you are going to run

away from me again, he thought.

Catherine asked him to take a chair near the fire. Both ladies sat waiting for him to make some conversation. It was somewhat unconventional to have him come visiting in the evening, and in the snow. He had better stick to something safe as conversation. Wasn't it quite proper that he should ask Miss St John about the school? He was now her employer, after all.

'How many children are there at the school?'

'We have twenty-two who come every day and nine children who attend when they can,' Miss St John answered.

He watched Miss Handscombe. Although her hair was pulled back severely behind her cap, a loose curl had escaped at the nape of her neck.

'And what is on the curriculum?'

Robert nodded, though he realised he had not heard the schoolteacher's answer. He had been regarding Miss Handscombe's dainty button nose and slender hands. The conversation seemed to have paused naturally. Noticing a shelf of books and a pile on the dresser whose spines told a mixture of histories and novels, he said, 'I see you enjoy reading, Miss St John.'

'Yes, indeed.'

'Perhaps you would find something of interest at the Park? The library is quite extensive, I believe.'

Now was the moment to press home his advantage.

'You both must come to the Park and use the library there.'

He guessed with her lively mind Lucinda would be a reader.

'Shall we say tomorrow, at two o'clock?'

He could see that, despite herself, something flickered in her eyes.

'Thank you, Your Grace,' Catherine said.

'Now that is agreed, I must bid you ladies good evening.'

Robert swept out of his chair and after giving a small bow, left before either had a chance to rise and show him to the door.

It continued to snow through the night. Lucinda stared out of the small window in her bedroom watching the fat, white flakes tumbling past. In the morning, everything would be covered in a fresh winter carpet.

If she described her confusion to herself it might seem clearer. The new Duke of Stanbridge had captured her attention from the moment he had come into the cottage until the moment he had left. The more she considered it, the more it came to her, that the fancy she had taken to Captain Monceaux, the dragoon, was not diminished by the same gentleman now being the Duke of Stanbridge.

It was impossible to fall in love with a handsome countenance or dashing uniform. She either loved the man himself, and it did not matter that he was a dragoon or a duke, or she did not love him. She knew only too well that she loved him . . .

Robert strode out across what were now his lawns, his boots making satisfying crunching sounds through the crisp snow. He had been informed that some parts of the garden were in need of work but the snow was a great leveller, hiding weed as well as flower.

The whitened lawns swept down from the house, guided by ancient-looking box hedging and not ending until the park began. It was a good few minutes' walk from the house to the end of the lawns where there was a small, round folly made of sandstone, with a domed, slate roof. It was reminiscent, he supposed, of a classical temple. He turned on his heels and headed back to the house.

He was a busy man these days. If his campaign was to win Lucinda Hand-scombe's heart he would now do it properly. Back inside, he smiled as the warmth, even in the draughty hall, hit him.

'Archer!' he bellowed.

Archer was the butler and had turned out to be the most useful chap in the whole house.

'Your Grace?' Archer appeared as if from nowhere.

'Skates, or at least blades — do we have any?'

'For ice skating, sir?'

'Of course!'

'Miss Harriett used to skate,' Archer muttered as he went away to do his master's bidding.

Miss Harriett, as Robert had learned quickly, was his mother. The fact that some thirty years ago she had married a wealthy Irish peer and was now Lady Monceaux seemed to have passed the servants at Wednesley Park by.

It was barely ten minutes after Robert had settled himself in front of the roaring fire that Archer returned with a dark, leather box. Damp had caused the leather to flake at the corners. Robert frowned, but inside the crumbling casket were half a dozen pairs of skating blades.

The ladies arrived at the Park promptly at two o'clock. Robert found them in the hall, prim, heavy-cloaked and booted.

'Miss St John, Miss Handscombe, I am delighted.'

He bent most particularly over her hand, pleased to find it quivered at his touch.

'Miss Handscombe, Archer will show you into the library where I expect you will want to begin a thorough examination of the volumes therein.'

'Thank you, Your Grace.'

'Miss St John, I have a matter concerning the school I wish to discuss with you.'

Lucinda followed the butler down the wide corridor and into the library. He gave a small bow and withdrew. Where should her appraisal of this vast room begin? Each bookcase was nearly as tall as the ceiling.

There was a wooden ladder on a rail to reach the highest shelves. Lucinda sighed. Could she use the ladder to investigate the highest volumes or had she taken all leave of her senses? Was climbing a library ladder improper? She placed her hand on the side of the ladder and tried to shake it. It didn't move. It was secure on its rails and had a metal bracket at its foot to fix it to the floor. She climbed up to the top easily, and her decision had been entirely the right one because at the top of the ladder, to the left, was an entire shelf of works by Shakespeare. Every play she had ever heard of was there and, bound in red leather, a slim volume of Mr Shakespeare's sonnets!

'Miss Handscombe? Ah, I see, a diligent start already.'

Lucinda's hand slipped, sending a book crashing to the ground. She started and clung to the ladder. That voice could belong to no-one else. She didn't dare turn around. Her cheeks were burning.

'Are you in need of any assistance?'

'No, I . . . '

She could hear him walking closer. They were quite alone in the room.

'What's this?'

She heard him pick up the book up

from the floor and the rustle of paper as he flicked through its pages.

'Mr Shakespeare's sonnets? How interesting. I am not that well versed in Mr Shakespeare's work myself but let me see. Ah, yes, here it is. Let me not to the marriage of true minds admit impediments.'

The way he said, marriage, as if . . . Oh, she didn't know. Lucinda shut her eyes.

'Mr Shakespeare appears rather optimistic as to the human condition. There are often impediments to marriage are there not, Miss Handscombe?'

'Yes . . . yes, there are.'

'The question is if in the case of a marriage for love such impediments have any validity.'

He was confusing her. She did not know what to say lest her words ended up saying more than she meant.

'I am not sure I know what you mean, Your Grace.'

He laughed and she heard the book thud shut.

'You are getting light in the head up that high! Are you not coming down? Can I tempt you with some refreshments?'

Lucinda made her way back down the ladder carefully, gripping it tightly, her heart pounding. Was there something else to his smile than polite kindness, something that made her tremor and lose all sense and conversation?

His eyes fixed on her countenance and then most particularly on her lips. She felt heat rise from her chest and up her neck to enflame her cheeks. She brushed at her skirts with her hand.

9

Robert broke the spell by turning and walking away. Her confusion and distracted brushing down of her clothes was fast fanning his interest into desire. It struck at his control. He had never felt like this before.

Without doubt, he still wanted her as his wife, but how to win her?

'May I escort you to the drawing-room. Miss St John is there already, partaking, I believe, of some lemonade.'

Her smile was quite guileless and unwittingly she had him captured again. The drawing-room at Wednesley Park in truth required repairs and new furnishings picked by somebody with an eye for fashion. Lucinda sat down as bid, in silence, gazing quite openly about her.

After a minute or two, brought back down to earth by the rattle of tea cups as Miss St John did the honours of pouring the tea, Robert said matter-of-factly, 'Miss Handscombe was captivated by the library.'

'Yes, it is a splendid library,' Lucinda answered and folded her hands in her lap. 'Quite an adventure to be had in there.'

'There are very few adventures to be had in Wednesley, Your Grace,' Miss St John said solemnly.

'Nonsense! I have an intention to try skating on the lake. Will you ladies join me?'

'We do not have any blades,' Miss Handscombe stated.

Robert smiled and called for Archer. The butler disappeared, reappearing a moment later with the shabby-looking box. He shook it over a corner of the carpet and out tumbled a dozen skating blades.

'So, shall we go skating?'

'Oh, yes, please,' Miss Handscombe replied, her eyes shining and her voice sounding like bells.

Robert caught her smile. He wanted it to always be like this.

On the ice, Lucinda knew that what she felt was envy. Catherine had taken to the ice like a duck to water. Lucinda had struggled to fasten the blades correctly to one of her boots. Robert had leaped to her assistance, brushed his hand against her ankles, disturbed her by his proximity. He had been so close she heard him breathing.

She was hesitant at first, but once she saw that he was busy with his own speed dashes and frightening jumps and halts, and that Catherine was trying out some manoeuvres of her own, she found her feet and started to glide across the lake at a respectable pace.

'You cut a fine figure on the ice, Miss Handscombe,' the duke said as he skated over to her.

Lucinda looked up, started and lost her footing on a rough patch of ice. She felt her balance desert her. She was going to hit the ground, hard. She hit something softer, halfway. He caught her! The sensation of his warm body was an even greater shock than any sheet of ice.

'I have got you,' he said.

His arms held her steady and she found herself looking into the eyes of a man who looked exactly as if he might kiss her. She wanted him to kiss her!

He did not, of course, kiss her or make any other move and when she dared to look back at him his expression was impenetrable.

'I'm all right, thank you, Your Grace.'

Why did she still feel cheated? She had wanted to stay safe in those warm arms for ever!

★ ★ ★

'Ockbourn House is shut, sir,' the housekeeper said and began to shut the door.

'Ockbourn House?' Rawleigh said in his most charming voice.

He had no intention of having his visit remarked upon.

'I am afraid I have come to the wrong place! Good day to you, madam.'

He turned on his heels and headed directly back to his curricle.

Ockbourn was to have been his salvation. The house was a Queen Anne masterpiece straight out of a pattern book and the Ockbourn estate held some of the finest arable land in Hertfordshire. Robert Monceaux, Duke of Stanbridge, had double crossed him, not paid him the money and he was staring at the prospect of ending up bankrupt and in prison before the month was out if he didn't do something. The deal was off and Miss Handscombe had disappeared into thin air. She was not here. But he knew where Stanbridge would be —Wednesley.

'I hear that Lady Monceaux and the duke's sisters have arrived this after-noon at Wednesley Park,' Catherine said as she came in through the door.

Lucinda's mouth felt dry. The duke's family was here! She did not want to begin to think on that and pulled herself back to listen.

'Now, do you want to borrow my sprigged muslin? They are likely to ask you to dine.'

But they didn't. No note or letter arrived.

The Park was less than a mile away but it might as well have been one hundred. Robert had come to see her yesterday, the day after she had fallen ice-skating, but she had said she was indisposed and now, today, nothing.

Of course, why would a duke invite a penniless orphan to dine and meet his family? He wouldn't. If only fate had left him a captain. But then he could not have afforded to marry.

Lucinda drove her face into her wet pillow and willed sleep to come . . .

Robert strode into the library and poured himself a glass of brandy from the decanter. He wasn't usually for strong liquor but it might help clear the fog in his mind. The hasty way Lucinda had flown out of his house after the skating incident still smote at his conscience, and that was two days ago.

She had been indisposed when he called yesterday afternoon, and then today, he'd been busy with the unexpected arrival of his mother and sisters, and quite unable to sneak out of the house.

If he stopped chasing her would she come to him? How long would he have to wait, or would she run away again? Robert put the glass down on the table. He didn't really want it. He would go to her again, tomorrow . . .

In a comfortable chair in his club, Boodles, in the west-end of London, Rodney Spiers sat reading an advertisement in the London Gazette.

The public is informed that the location of a young lady of the name HANDSCOMBE is most urgently sought. All information gratefully received by Mr Tindal, Solicitor, Lincoln's Inn.

Rupert cast the newspaper aside. Handscombe — that was a name he had not heard in a long while. John Handscombe had been one of his best friends at school. A regular out-and-outer Handscombe, he had felt his loss keenly. One minute he had been envious of John going off and seeing the world. The next, he had been relieved it had not been himself drowned at such a tragically young age.

As if it were some pre-ordained moment, Rodney Spiers looked up and saw the older, yet, unmistakably familiar figure of John Handscombe walk into the room!

'Rodney?' The man's brow creased. 'Rodney Spiers? Is it you?'

'John!' Rodney cried leaping up from his chair.

John Handscombe was older, of course, but his firm jaw-line and blonde hair were unmistakable.

'John! We all thought you were at the bottom of the ocean!'

'Well, I am not, as you can see.'

'I don't know what to say. Have you come far?'

'You could say that,' John replied with his famous smile, 'but lately, only from Bristol.'

'Come,' Rodney instructed, 'sit down and you can tell me where on earth you have been hiding these last few years.'

'That story,' John replied as he took a chair, 'will have to wait. I have a much more pressing matter I must ask your assistance.'

'Whatever I can do, I shall.'

'Thank you,' John replied with obvious relief in his voice. 'It has been difficult to know where to turn. I have been away for so long, and, as you say, given up for dead.'

'Funny thing actually,' Spiers replied. 'Have you seen today's Gazette?'

John shook his head.

Rodney leaned over to the small table just behind him, found the paper he had only just cast aside and rustled through it to the right page.

John's face paled as he read the advertisement.

'My sister! Lucinda! I had better go

to the solicitor directly.'

'I will come with you.'

Meanwhile, some distance away, Rawleigh cursed under his breath and tore the page from the newspaper, throwing it quickly in the library fire. An advertisement! Not only the immediate danger of Lucinda finding out the truth but an open invitation to every fortune hunter in Christendom to join the search for her. They would have to move today. There had been two options. Abduct her himself or find some ruffians to do it for him. Ruffians, however, required payment, so he had chosen to do it himself, with Cunningham's assistance.

Cunningham had observed that Lucinda was wont to take a walk in the mornings along a path that led past the old common on one side and a field known as Five Acres on the other, then turning past Hadley's Wood to get back into the village. There were no roads into Five Acres and the common was accessible only by horse or on foot.

However, it was possible to bring a light carriage along the woodcutters' track that led into Hadley's Wood. The vehicle would be at hand, yet hidden. There were places for them to hide so she could be surprised and it was far enough from the village that nothing would be heard . . .

The sun was shining, the snow melting. It was a little warmer today. As Lucinda walked, she spied a robin hopping about on the glistening bright snow but it didn't make her smile. If only she could sort out her thoughts!

Lucinda shrieked as a man suddenly jumped out of the wood and stood directly in front of her. He was wearing a huge black cloak with a hood that partially obscured his face. Lucinda wanted to run, but for the moment was frozen still as the man approached and addressed her.

'Do not be afraid,' he instructed.

She knew that voice!

'Lord Rawleigh?'

His was the same voice, too, she

suddenly realised, as the highwayman who had accosted them that day on Hounslow Heath! What was going on?

'You will come with me. You will not be harmed for I intend to marry you at the earliest opportunity. I have Mr Ferris's consent. Your position in Society as Lady Rawleigh will be secure.'

'Lord Rawleigh,' Lucinda said as fiercely as she could, her legs unable to move, 'I have no desire to marry you.'

At that moment, another man appeared from the wood and was advancing towards her with a big blanket. If they tied her up, she would never escape.

'I will come with you.'

She would escape at the first opportunity, she planned as he stepped forward and grasped her wrist.

'I dislike violence,' he said, 'but you have nothing to fear.'

Lucinda was led into the wood, and was strangely relieved that a curricle was waiting close by. It meant that perhaps Lord Rawleigh spoke the truth and that this was to be a properly executed abduction not something far, far worse. As long as she remained unbound, she could outwit them.

But the man with the blanket, who was he?

Lord Rawleigh opened the door to the curricle. No-one was holding the reins. She had never handled a carriage before but these were well-behaved horses. If she stayed calm, they might just listen to her. Lucinda grabbed the reins, tumbling forward as she flicked them urgently. The horses, unsure of their driver, at first did not move. Lord Rawleigh shouted and lunged forward to grasp the back wheel, and the other man was running towards them.

Go, Lucinda willed the horses. For goodness' sake, go!

The horses moved forward but only a pace. Lord Rawleigh still held the back wheel. Then, from somewhere close by in the wood, came shouting. Suddenly, the duke was hurtling towards her. As he emerged from the trees, the man dropped his blanket and ran. Robert stopped before he had quite reached her. Lucinda saw the indecision in his eyes, felt it hurt her. She looked away and tried to comfort herself with the thought that he had rescued her, again.

Lucinda winced at the white anger which flashed across his face and she swelled with pride at his ability to control it as he faced her abductor.

'What now?' Lord Rawleigh said, still holding the wheel.

'You're lucky I am not hauling you before the justice of the peace to have you thrown straight into gaol.'

Lord Rawleigh did not reply.

'Abducting young ladies isn't exactly what I would have expected of a peer of the realm. Then again, you haven't exactly been honest with me and I heard you lost a king's ransom at the tables.' Robert's eyes narrowed. 'Come on, then, what was it drove you to this act? Money?'

Lord Rawleigh grimaced and stood up.

'I shall be bankrupted now.'

'Why Miss Handscombe, or is there something I have not been told?'

Lucinda stared at the duke but he did not look at her.

'A damn fine state of affairs!'

Robert had started to pace backwards and forwards. He stopped about five paces in front of Lord Rawleigh.

'I am only newly ennobled and not yet had a chance to learn all the rules. However, you are a lord and I am a duke and I expect we can work something out to keep you out of prison but if I ever hear of you trying to pull a stunt like this again there will be the devil to pay.'

'I would prefer it if we could work something out.'

The horses reared, whinnied and plunged forward. Lucinda was thrown back. She pulled the reins as hard as she could, tried to blink away the biting rush of cold air, but to no avail. They were not stopping. They took themselves down the track, out of the wood.

She pulled again but the horses kept going, kicking through the slush with a vengeance, dragging her around the corner, off the track and on to the road. The curricle leaned. She slid downwards, to the right, hitting the cushions with force. She forced her eyes to stay open.

10

At last the horses began to slow, tire. How long had they been going? Not more than an hour. How far had they come? For five miles, or maybe ten, they had been pelting along the road.

Lucinda's arms felt as though they had been nearly wrenched from her. She could see some cottages up ahead, then the swinging sign of an inn. The ostler there regarded her exactly as she would expect an ostler who had watched a lone gentlewoman tool a dashing curricle into his yard.

'Thank you, my good man,' she said and handed him the reins and walked into the inn as if she went into inns every day of her life. But which door to take? She was in a small, low hallway with a door to the left and one to the right.

'Can I help you?' A man appeared. The innkeeper?

'Yes, is there somewhere I can rest while I wait for my husband to arrive? I came on a little ahead.'

She couldn't be that far away from Wednesley, so she could send a note to Catherine.

'Yes, Mrs . . . Mrs?'

'Smith.'

'Mrs Smith, would you like any refreshment?'

'Yes, please, hot chocolate, and I must write an urgent letter.'

The innkeeper nodded and led her into a small sitting-room. She sat by the fire. Catherine would know what to do, perhaps get Mr Adams the parson to drive here. The innkeeper returned shortly and set the writing materials down on the small table.

'Where am I?' she asked him.

'Ockbourn.'

She scribbled a quick note to Catherine but she did not even have any money to send the letter. When the innkeeper returned with her hot drink she pressed the letter on him, but he looked at her suspiciously.

'Have you run away?'

'Of course not! My husband will be along shortly. Please have this letter sent without delay. In the meantime, I shall go for a short walk.'

She must try and forget Robert. She had built her feelings for him up to be such a great thing, that she looked for return in his every gesture, read things into his every move, every word, imagining things that weren't there.

As she walked, she had the odd feeling that Ockbourn, like Wednesley had been, was familiar to her, the way the houses were positioned, the white-washed gables of the cottage opposite, the pond beside the green. Was she so desperate to belong somewhere that she now imagined it everywhere she went?

She opened the lychgate and wandered into the churchyard. Out of the corner of her eye, in a very sheltered spot, in the lee of the church, she saw a single snowdrop hidden behind two gravestones. Lucinda went over and bent down to examine it more closely. In the corner of her eye, she noticed the inscription on one of the nearby gravestones — IAH HANDSC . . .

She looked at it more closely but some lichen was partially obscuring the text. She found a piece of stone and scratched at the lichen. As more letters were revealed she gasped and stumbled back. The surname was clear to see — HANDSCOMBE! She swung around at the crunching sound of footsteps. It was none other than the duke! Her hand flew to her mouth.

'Are you all right, Miss Handscombe?' Robert asked.

'Yes, thank you. She felt her chest constrict.

'If you are sure, please put me out of my misery and tell me what on earth you were doing to that poor gravestone?'

'Look,' she said, pointing, and watched while he read the partial inscription she had uncovered and looked back at her.

'Do you think it might be a relative?'

'Well, at the moment, I can't even read the whole of it.'

'Allow me.'

He reached forward and his hand moved towards hers. She dropped the flint into his palm. He made short work of scraping away the rest of the lichen, to uncover the full inscription — **JOSIAH HANDSCOMBE, DIED 1782, and his beloved wife, MARY, DIED 1785.**

She continued staring at the stone.

'So do you think they might be relatives?' he asked.

'I do not know,' Lucinda replied with a shake of her head.

He seized her hands and, before she could pull away, held them enclosed in his, protectively. She raised her eyes to his. She remembered looking at his eyes that first time she had ever seen him on Hounslow Heath. She could not pull her hands away — she wanted him to hold them, warm, safe.

'So, what are you doing here?' she said eventually.

'Well,' he said with a grimace, 'I was right in the middle of rescuing a young lady when she bolted. I had to return home to get Armada, thus the delay, but it was easy enough to trail a young lady dashing into Hertfordshire in sole charge of a curricle.'

He looked strangely immovable, as if he was happy to stand there all day talking to her in the churchyard, and he still held her hands.

'Miss Handscombe, although you appear to be completely impervious to my finer feelings, I have nevertheless come to care for you.'

'I need to try to find out about Josiah Handscombe. I have no family, you see, and . . . '

His kiss finished the sentence for her. His warm figure pressed her against him, shielded her from the cold. The deafening sound of the church bells made her jump back. The duke was straightening his cravat.

'I shall make enquiries about Josiah Handscombe. If he died less than thirty

158

years ago there will be people here who knew him. It will be easier for me to ask than you.'

'Thank you, Your Grace.'

'It would please me greatly if you would call me Robert. Shall we return to the inn?' he said, brushing the back of her hand with his lips, making her quiver again. 'I believe we need to collect the curricle you stole and I will settle the bill before taking you home.'

Home? Whose home? For one foolish moment, she imagined that he might have come after her out of more than a sense of duty. No! She banished that hope immediately. Yet why had he kissed her? To comfort her? A strange comfort, indeed, that sent her heart racing and the blood pounding through every part of her. The danger would be if she weakened, for if she demonstrated her vulnerability again, it might draw him to act on his good instincts again. Her thoughts were too mixed up to think rationally on the whole subject.

Back in the room at the inn, Robert

joined her, having settled affairs with the landlord. The door closed with a determined thud. Lucinda looked up and caught the flicker of his eyes as he came to sit beside her.

'I have something to tell you,' he said. 'Lord Rawleigh has told me everything. You are an heiress, a considerable heiress, with a vast fortune from your late uncle, Mr John Handscombe.'

'Uncle?'

She had never heard of an uncle. But he was dead, this uncle whom she had never known, Mr John Handscombe. A lump grew in her throat. He would have been her papa's brother.

'Your father and his elder brother were estranged, so I believe.'

Pain tore at her chest and her throat constricted. It was difficult to breathe and every breath was desperate to break into a sob.

'You understand what this means, don't you, Lucinda?'

She shook her head, knowing that a tear had broken free and was running down her cheek. She'd found her family and lost them. What now? She had no answer.

'You have found your family, and you may do exactly as you choose. I understand the fortune you have left you will make you one of the richest ladies in England. There will be no need for you ever to earn a living,' he continued but she had little wish to listen. 'And there is a fine house, newly built by your uncle.'

'House?'

He had pulled a handkerchief from his pocket and placed it in her hand. She wiped it across her eyes.

'Where? You must tell me everything you know, please. Where is it, the house?'

Robert looked away and she heard him expel a slow breath. Puzzled, she reached towards him, ventured to lay her hand on his, and repeated her simple question. His answer was no louder than a whisper.

'Here. Here, in Ockbourn, although

the landlord tells me that Ockbourn House is two miles from the village. I am sure we will discover that Josiah Handscombe from the churchyard is a relative. Do you know anything of a lady called Mrs Hodges, Mrs Hodges of Bath?' he asked.

'She was a friend of my mother.'

'And of mine, and she would have known Lady Hastings?'

'Very likely. I think they were all at school together. Mrs Hodges looked after me after my parents were lost.'

Suddenly everything was fitting together. She could see a way ahead. She had a home, somewhere where there had been Handscombes, where Handscombes belonged.

'Are you all right?'

'Yes,' she replied and stood up, moving towards him.

He covered the distance between them in a moment, in two paces, and was reaching towards her. She had to say what she wanted to say, quickly.

'It is not that I haven't come to care

for you, Robert, but I cannot marry a duke.'

'I am still Captain Monceaux, as a courtesy title.'

'You are also the Duke of Stanbridge. How can I possibly be the wife of so illustrious a personage?'

'Stuff and nonsense,' he said. 'If I took you in my arms now you would relent immediately.'

'It is that I don't ... that I won't ...'

'Don't what, Lucinda?'

He let her hand fall gently and raised his hands to cup her face lightly.

'May I have your permission to call you by your given name, wife?'

'But I am not your wife!'

'No, not yet.' Robert smiled.

Lucinda looked at him, caught the twist of pain in his eyes.

'It may have escaped your notice,' he said, 'but I have not yet asked you to marry me.'

He came forward and bent down on one knee before her. He drew her hands and held them clasped in his own.

'Lucinda, will you consent to promise yourself to this impatient knight? He wants you for his wife so dreadfully.'

'I will, but . . . '

'No buts!'

He clasped her hands more tightly.

'We must arrange it immediately.'

'There must be a but. I am not twenty-one until June.'

'June it will be then, though how I will bear the wait, I do not know.'

He smiled, rose now and drew her easily into his arms. How could she resist falling into his embrace? A small suspicion had formed and however much she willed it, it would not go away. Exactly how long had he known that she was an heiress?

Lucinda gulped back the lump in her throat. The air had got heavier. She did not want to say it and yet she had to. She had to know.

'Robert, when did you know I was an heiress?'

'Today,' he said immediately, then

added, 'and I am mightily glad I did not know before or I would never have had the courage to catch you. I'm fairly flush in the pockets these days, I'll have you know, wench, before you start getting any ideas you can lord it over me.'

The spark in his eyes was irresistible and guileless. Robert had loved her when she had been poor and now she was an heiress it had not made a jot of difference.

'I love you, Robert,' she said at last.

'Have I told you I love you?'

'Not exactly.'

Her heart silenced her fears and every inch of her surrendered to him as he kissed her again.

'Come,' he said at last, 'let's to Ockbourn House!'

★ ★ ★

Robert brought the curricle to a halt and suddenly the prospect of facing the red-brick house was daunting. Who lived here now? Could she really just go up and knock on the door?

'This is the house I remember,' she said.

There was no sign of any groom or other person to take care of them. She looked at the large front door and then back to Robert, caught his eye and walked to him so that she stood right next to him. Confident that there was no doubt now that Robert loved her, she could not resist teasing him. She frowned.

'Are you sure I am the number one female in your affections?'

He looked at her, puzzled.

'Of course.'

'Even before Armada?'

His eyebrows raised and then his eyes narrowed. He drew in a long breath. He caught her in a masterful kiss and pulled her towards him. She was aware of the creak of the door opening but it was some faraway place.

'Sir! Unhand my sister at once, or I will not vouch for the consequences!'

Robert sprung apart from his beloved. Confound it! What ill-luck to have been caught. Lucinda would no doubt be blushing. A young gentleman stood framed by the darkness of the doorway.

Hang on, had the man just said sister? Robert glanced from one to the other. The gentleman's countenance was gripped with anger, Lucinda's white as chalk.

'John?'

Lucinda's voice was low. Her eyes were screwed up as if she was not seeing properly the man who had spoken. He raced down the steps.

'Lucinda, it is me, your brother, John.'

'But I thought . . . ' Her voice was little more than a whisper now, her face pale, drained of emotion.

11

I did not drown.' Her brother's face creased. 'I was lucky. Suffice to say, I survived. It's a long story. I hate to mar this moment I have looked forward to for so long, dear sister. But what the devil do you think you are doing kissing this man in common view of anyone who might be passing? And who is he anyway?'

Every muscle in Robert's body tensed. He stood up straighter and wished some confounded groom would appear to take the horses.

'Robert Monceaux, Duke of Stanbridge,' he said, knowing but not regretting that his voice sounded as cold as ice.

'John, Robert and I are to be married,' Lucinda announced.

Robert's heart swelled. John Handscombe started and his lips quivered uneasily in response. Something had flashed across his eyes. Fear? It was clear he had not expected her to say that.

'Betrothed or not, I take exception to such wanton behaviour! Was he trying to seduce you? Do you realise I have today been to see your friend, Miss St John, frantic that you were missing, and then up to the Park where she thought you might have gone, only to find a madhouse, full of women lit up like lamps and whispering about bridal laces, because the duke, too, had disappeared, after my sister.'

Robert fought to keep a smile off his face. Handscombe had guessed then, but didn't like the stark confirmation Lucinda had given him.

'But no-one knew where! There was nothing I could do but come here, wait for word, hope that my sister was not already halfway to Gretna Green!' John's eyes flashed. 'I shall most certainly not grant my permission for any marriage unless I am completely satisfied that you desire my sister not for her fortune but for herself.'

Lucinda gazed in confusion at the house, its bricks glowing even in the cold, and the gentlemen standing before her — a home and family which could be hers.

'Sister, unfortunately this place is not habitable,' John was saying. 'We shall have to return directly to London.'

Yet behind her stood another gentleman, offering another home, another family. Lucinda clasped her hands around her waist and shivered. John was her brother. She had wanted at first to run to him, to embrace him.

'Lucinda?'

John stepped forward, not entirely sure. He held his arms out to her. He was her brother, wasn't he? He looked older and leaner somehow. Had the six years he had been away changed him into somebody unrecognisable?

Lucinda felt sick. Her empty stomach tightened, and fear stabbed her in a way that she had not even felt at Lord

Rawleigh's kidnap attempt. A shadow crossed John's eyes. She made herself take a step towards him, place her hands tentatively in his.

'John, I . . . '

She did not know what to say. He grasped her fingers, possessively. She quivered. Her brother was her guardian now, more potent a guardian than Mr Ferris would ever have been. He was responsible for her and able to dictate to her until she reached the proper age. Could she turn her back on her brother for another man?

She turned and looked to Robert, felt John's grip tighten. Robert caught her eye briefly and sent her a glance that began to reassure her.

'Let us return to the Park and talk about this,' he said. 'Mr Handscombe, you are welcome as my guest for as long as you wish.'

'Do I have solemn undertaking as a gentleman that I shall see you directly at the Park?'

'Yes, I give you my word.'

She hardly knew how she had got back into the curricle and that Robert had tucked the rug around her and was driving them away from Ockbourn House. She crushed a horrid thought that she could throw herself out of the curricle, now, before it gathered too much speed. She'd be bruised but she could run, run away somewhere.

No, she wasn't running away, wasn't even going to consider it. What she wanted now was both John and Robert.

'My mother, Lady Monceaux, and my three sisters are at Wednesley,' Robert said as they turned on to the road. 'Lorna, Bridget and Jane.'

Would they welcome her, Lucinda wondered. She wanted to ask him but his face was tight-set with concentration as he drove the horses at a lightning pace.

Now, as well as her brother, there were his mother and three sisters to thrust a knife into her happiness. She pulled her cloak more tightly around her. Should she have gone with John to

London after all?

She drew in a long breath. If it came to it, she would fight. She would rather try, and be humiliated, than walk away from the man she loved.

'Do not worry. It will all work out,' he said just then as if he had been able to read her thoughts.

She could think of no easy answer so she remained silent, tried to savour the moment of them being alone in the curricle, remember the heat of his kisses and everything about Robert that made him so perfect. She would have to trust him to sort out his own family but she needed to forge her own treaty with her brother.

They arrived at the Park all too quickly. The house was full of women, as John had said. Lucinda watched Robert stride ahead, sweep them out of the way with promises that he would attend to them directly, and usher her into the drawing-room. He planted a distracted kiss on her forehead and then Lucinda found she was alone.

She felt no compulsion to sit down. It suited her better to walk around the large room, to try and distract herself by looking at the curious objects in the display cabinets. So many snuff boxes, hateful little things, serving no useful purpose, gathering dust! They must be the collection of the old duke.

A pair of large, china vases, decorated in hunting scenes, sat on a pair of wooden jardinières. To be able to throw them at the display cabinet and break the snuff boxes into a thousand pieces would have suited her disposition!

Where was everyone now? She felt her fists clench together and heart begin to race. She'd had enough of being shut in rooms while elsewhere others made decisions without her being there. She walked purposefully towards the drawing-room door, seized the handle, turned it, pulled the door open — and came face to face with John, hand outstretched. He must have just been about to open the door himself. She stumbled backwards.

'Brother!'

John darted forward and caught her arm to steady her. There was no real danger that she would have lost her footing and Lucinda pulled away without thinking. He pulled his jacket straight, came in and shut the door, his countenance still stone.

'Sister, I have some news I must impart.'

Lucinda bit her lip, felt a lump stuck in her throat. She should not have pushed him away.

'If you mean I am an heiress, then I know.'

The door crashed open then and in flew Robert, slamming it immediately shut. He swept past John, past her, coat tails flying, and gestured towards the sofas in the middle of the room.

'Shall we sit down?'

Robert would sort it out, she thought. She trusted him.

John held her gaze as they went to sit down.

'Your parents, our parents,' he said,

'are dead, dearest sister. Only I survived the shipwreck. According to the laws of England, the family estate is mine.'

His voice was strangely light, gentle, although he stumbled over some of his words.

'I will do everything possible to ensure you have a substantial portion.'

Robert stretched his legs out in front of him as if this was an informal family gathering. He smiled at John.

'A portion is quite unnecessary on my account. I would be happy to provide for Lucinda.'

Why had he leaped in so soon? She and John were brother and sister but she was also Robert's. He turned his amiable gaze to her for a moment. John coughed into his sleeve, but didn't meet Robert in the eye as he spoke to her.

'If I do not stay in England, I will have Ockbourn House transferred wholly to you, dear sister.'

'Not stay in England, John? Where are you going?'

Her stomach clenched. How dare he

come back to her now, dictate his terms and then say that he was leaving again?

His eyes turned away from her.

'I have not decided yet.'

'John, I have only just found you again. What happened exactly?'

'It is a long story.'

Out of the corner of her eye, Lucinda saw Robert stiffen. She hoped it was because he wished to pay attention, not because of something else, like jealousy. He had no need to be jealous.

'I was lucky enough to be taken in by a plantation owner,' John said. 'He did not know who I was, nor did I at first, but it was clear I was an English gentleman. I didn't even remember the shipwreck. I could have asked him to pay for my passage home earlier, but I tell you, I did not know until about a year ago what there was for me here.'

John looked at her as if to say he was sorry. She smiled in return, accepted his unspoken apology. She had only ever faced the shipwreck in her dreams, but he had lived it, lived through it.

'It seemed easier to stay away, to try and forget, but then I knew I couldn't,' he continued. 'I had to come back if only to see my sister and assure myself that she was safe, well and happy. But I hardly know yet whether I want to be John Handscombe, of Ockbourn House, Hertfordshire, or whether I shall go back to the Indies.'

'You must stay! I mean, will you stay, at least, for a while?'

Lucinda wrung her hands in her lap, rounded every word so there could be no doubt as to its meaning. This was an appeal, her brother had to understand.

'And I am safe, well and happy. In fact, I have never been happier.'

'I will stay for a little while,' John conceded.

'John,' Lucinda changed her tone of voice to one which was stronger, 'I have never been happier because I am in love with Robert and he loves me, and we are to be married. Please don't insist that you disapprove.'

Robert felt his breath catch. The ties

were binding now. She was demanding something of her brother, not just he of her. Robert's every muscle tensed.

'From the moment he first saw me, Robert has been kind and gallant, escorting me to safety, protecting me,' she said. 'His every action has been kindness. He had looked out for me as steadfastly as any brother or guardian. Had you been there you would have done the same.'

She cast her eyes down on to her lap, but only for a moment. They flashed up again, and this time the fire was unmistakable, warning him not to defy her.

'I love him, John, in a way I cannot describe. It is too important to be risked, too all consuming to be cast aside. I will not do it. No, John, I will not do it, even if you get down on your hands and knees and ask me. You might take me away from Robert and then go back to the Indies, and leave me with nobody.'

Robert felt his breast swell, with

pride, love and the prospect becoming surer with every minute that love would triumph. He had no right to interrupt but Handscombe still had not spoken. He was looking uneasy and pale in the face. Robert knew how he felt about his own sisters. Handscombe was to be pitied for being issued such a challenge, deserved or not.

Lucinda was blinking furiously as if at any moment she might break down and cry. Robert could say his words better standing up, so he did and placed himself with his back to the fire.

'It is not to be envied, having to choose between a husband and a brother, nor is it to face the prospect of losing a sister to a rogue. Handscombe, if you give your permission that we might be married, I give you my word as a gentleman that there is no coercion here. I do not desire a penny. Lucinda is my only object.'

Handscombe was listening, carefully. He cast his eyes around the room, caught her gaze, and then Robert's.

Robert felt his muscles relax.

'Lucinda, is this what you want?' John asked.

She rose from her chair and flew towards him, clasping his hands in her own.

'John, yes. Please, say yes!'

Handscombe's face twisted. Lucinda did not leave his side, waiting for his reply. At last his mouth curved upwards into a grin.

'I hear you, sister. There is nothing else I can say except that in the face of such determination, I insist you marry immediately!'

Lucinda pressed herself against him as he rose, planting kisses on her brother's cheek. He stepped back at first, embarrassed, but her victory was complete and he embraced her, holding her close to him.

'Oh, Lucinda, I thought I had lost you completely.'

Robert wanted to take her into his arms but knew he had to wait. When it was his turn, he swept Lucinda into his arms, crushed her to him, planted the briefest of kisses, branded her his, his one true love. He had thought himself her champion but she was willing to risk all to champion him.

Lady Hastings came for their wedding and so it seemed did half of Society. Some had been lured by the news of Stanbridge's three beautiful sisters, but for the most part, Lucinda suspected if was curiosity that had unusually lured them out of town in the middle of the Season. It was the wedding of the missing heiress of what had been called a notorious deception.

As they left the churchyard husband and wife, Robert took her hand, smoothed it in his own, teasing her fingers on to his arm and then resting his other hand on top.

'I love you,' he whispered, tying her gaze to his own.

Robert's eyes burned into hers with an ardour that was unextinguishable and Lucinda found herself shamefully longing for the moment when they would be alone.

It was said that for a bride truly in love, her wedding day was the happiest of her life. It had been perfect. Catherine had looked beautiful as her maid of honour, and with her brother, John, to give her away, she knew there could be no happier woman in the world!

The End

Other titles in the
Linford Romance Library:

LOVE'S DAWNING

Diney Delancey

Rosanne Charlton joins her friend Ruth and family for a holiday in Southern Ireland. Unfortunately, the holiday is marred for her by the arrival of Ruth's brother, Brendan O'Neill, whom Rosanne has always disliked. However, Brendan's presence is not Rosanne's only problem . . . Trouble and danger close round her, like an Irish mist, when she becomes unwittingly involved in mysterious activities in the bay — and finds herself fighting for survival in the dark waters of the Atlantic.

BETRAYAL OF INNOCENCE

Valerie Holmes

Annie works hard to keep her father from the poorhouse. However, she is wracked with guilt as she watches her friend, Georgette Davey, being used by Lady Constance. Annie longs to escape her life at the Hall, taking Georgette with her — but how? The arrival of the mysterious doctor, Samuel Speer, adds to her dilemma as Annie's concern for her friend grows. Georgette's innocence has been betrayed, but Annie is unaware of the threat that hangs over her own.